He couldn't

Having dinner al[   ]
hadn't been such[   ]
find out more abo[   ]such
an intriguing dicho[   ]y of cool professionalism and
heated sensuality.

"This is great," Jilly said. "We can sit here and drink
wine until we really like each other. A couple of dozen
bottles ought to do it." After gracing him with a quick
grin, she returned her attention to the menu.

Couple of dozen bottles? *Ha ha.* Had he just
found her alluring? Surely he'd meant that she
was a smart-ass. And how come she wasn't having
any problem ignoring him, while he felt aroused and
flustered? He'd always been so cool, detached and in
control. That is, until the mix-up when he'd found *her*
in his hotel room wearing only black satin lingerie.

Well, sexual frustration definitely loved company, and
he was tired of suffering alone. She couldn't possibly
be as calm and collected as she clearly wanted him
to believe.

And it was about time he did something about it.

Dear Reader,

In my house, the unexpected is a frequent occurrence—
with varying degrees of good and bad. "Good unexpected"
is when my husband announces that he's taking us to our
favorite restaurant for dinner. Or when I discover a forgotten
dollar bill in the bottom of my purse. "Bad unexpected" is
stuff that follows the words *uh-oh*, like when my son said,
"Uh-oh, I think I put too much detergent in the washing
machine." (You don't want to know what happened.)
Or when I said, "Uh-oh—I don't think all that smoke is
supposed to be coming out of the oven." (Although this
did lead to "good unexpected" when my husband took
us to our favorite restaurant.) But we all know that any
kind of "unexpected" is hard to handle during the holidays.

Matt Davidson experiences a major case of "bad unexpected"
when he arrives at a posh resort to schmooze an important
client, only to discover that Jilly Taylor, his biggest rival,
has already checked in. *We* know "bad unexpected" can
sometimes lead to "good unexpected," but Jilly and Matt
will just have to find that out for themselves....

I love to hear from readers! You can contact me through
my Web site at www.JacquieD.com, where you can enter
my monthly contest and find out about my latest releases.

Happy holidays!

Jacquie D'Alessandro

Books by Jacquie D'Alessandro

HARLEQUIN TEMPTATION
917—IN OVER HIS HEAD

JACQUIE D'ALESSANDRO

A SURE THING?

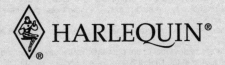
HARLEQUIN®

TORONTO • NEW YORK • LONDON
AMSTERDAM • PARIS • SYDNEY • HAMBURG
STOCKHOLM • ATHENS • TOKYO • MILAN • MADRID
PRAGUE • WARSAW • BUDAPEST • AUCKLAND

This book is lovingly dedicated to my Uncle Bill and Aunt Gwen Johnston. Thank you for all your love
and support, and for the many happy memories of fun times spent together. Those first two weeks
of August on Long Island and our holidays in Maine were always so special.

And as always, to my wonderful husband, Joe, for the love and laughter he brings to my life,
and my terrific son, Christopher, aka Love and Laughter, Jr. I'll never forget the special day
of fun we had researching this book—especially the CCM.

Acknowledgments
Thank you to Charles Massoud, owner of Paumanok Vineyards,
Wendy Turbush, Bill Bladykas of the Love Lane Sweet Shoppe,
and the kind people at Raphael, Lenz Winery and Pugliese Vineyards
for answering my many questions and for making such delicious wines.
Thanks also to Brenda Chin, Steven Axelrod, Damaris Rowland,
Wendy Etherington, Jenni Grizzle, Lea and Art D'Alessandro,
and Kay and Jim Johnson.

ISBN 0-373-69154-8

A SURE THING?

Copyright © 2003 by Jacquie D'Alessandro.

This edition published by arrangement with Harlequin Books S.A.

® and TM are trademarks of the publisher. Trademarks indicated with
® are registered in the United States Patent and Trademark Office, the
Canadian Trade Marks Office and in other countries.

Visit us at www.eHarlequin.com

Printed in U.S.A.

Prologue

WINNING A ONE HUNDRED MILLION dollar ad campaign. Now *that* would be one hell of a Christmas present.

Adam Terrell, CEO of Maxximum Advertising, pressed the button to disconnect his call, rose from the chair behind his curved granite desk, and barely refrained from indulging in an undignified end-zone type victory dance.

The chance for Maxximum to represent ARC Software in its new ad campaign was definitely not a bad way to start off the day. The account wasn't yet in the bag, but as he'd just learned during his phone conversation with Jack Witherspoon, ARC's CEO, Maxximum was one of the agencies on the short list.

"And it's my job to make sure Maxximum is the *only* agency left on that list," Adam murmured to himself.

Unable to remain still, he crossed the wide expanse of pale blue carpet to his huge office windows. From the vantage point of his tenth-floor, Madison Avenue office, he stared down at the busy street below. Pedestrians, their collars pulled up against the blustery winter cold and lingering snow flurries, trudged along the busy Manhattan street, many laden down with colorful holiday shopping bags, vaguely reminding Adam that only ten days remained until Christmas. There was no doubt about what he wanted sitting under his tree—a contract with Jack Witherspoon's signature.

But since Maxximum wasn't the only firm vying for the account, he needed an edge. Something to make Maxximum stand out. And he didn't have much time. Witherspoon wanted an ad campaign in place before his next shareholders meeting. Adam needed his best and brightest on this.

Two names instantly popped into his head. Matt Davidson and Jillian Taylor. Both were openly ambitious, exceptionally talented and creative, and able to focus on their jobs with single-minded concentration and determination. And both were highly competitive—especially with each other. They circled each other like two wary fighters in the ring, and had done so since Matt joined Maxximum a year ago and promptly landed the Strattford Furniture account—a company Jilly had been courting for several weeks. The gauntlet had been thrown, and over the past year, Adam had watched with calculated interest how Jilly and Matt constantly tried to outdo each other. Sure, their rivalry brought tension to the office, but who cared? It also brought results, with Maxximum the big winner. If Jilly couldn't bring in a particular client, then Matt could, and visa versa.

"Jilly and Matt," he mused. "Yeah..." If he sent them both after ARC, no doubt *one* of them would land the account. And if there was one thing Adam liked, especially where hundred-million-dollar accounts were concerned, it was a sure thing.

Of course, Jilly and Matt wouldn't like it. Last summer Adam had purposely pitted them against each other for the Lone Star Steaks account, certain that one of them would win it for Maxximum. And Jilly had succeeded, with a brilliant campaign fired by her determination to beat her nemesis.

Adam had shrugged off their displeasure at his tactics.

Sure, it was devious. But the only way to survive in the cutthroat world of advertising was to wield a sharper machete than the next guy. He sure as hell hadn't built Maxximum from a start-up company to one of the best ad agencies in New York in under ten years without a little bloodshed. But perhaps the smartest strategy would be to make sure Jilly and Matt didn't realize they'd been squared off against each other again until it was too late....

One corner of Adam's mouth lifted. After crossing to his desk, he picked up the phone. A little bit more blood was about to be shed.

1

MATT DAVIDSON EXITED Adam Terrel's office, closed the heavy oak door behind him and awarded himself a mental high-five. *Yes!* He'd waited a long time for a chance like this, and he had full confidence in his creative ability to land the ARC account. *Goodbye, cubicle—hellooo multi-windowed corner office. And hellooo promotion, raise, bonus and perks, too.*

His mind already buzzing with ideas, he made his way toward the desk of Adam's secretary, Debra. Per Adam's instructions, Matt needed to get the number of Maxximum's travel agent from Debra, then book himself a room at Chateau Fontaine for this weekend. Adam had already arranged a suite for Jack Witherspoon at the Chateau—one of Long Island's most exclusive resorts, built on the property of the Fontaine Winery—the perfect place to schmooze wine aficionado Jack. Jack had even cleared his calendar for Monday, affording Matt an extra day to reel in his fish. Between the winery, the five-star restaurant, wine tastings, cigar bar, spa, indoor pool and luxurious rooms, Matt didn't doubt for a minute that ARC would sign with Maxximum.

When he arrived at her desk, Debra was on a call. She smiled, held up her index finger to indicate she'd only be a minute, then returned her attention to her computer screen. Matt nodded and leaned his back against the white marble pillar near Debra's desk. A cheerful holiday song lauding the joys of a winter wonderland filtered softly from the recessed stereo speakers. Casting his gaze around, Matt noted the blink of twinkling lights adorning the six-foot Christmas tree in the corner near the bank of windows, a colorful reminder that time was running short to complete his Christmas shopping. He still needed to pick up a DVD player for his sister and brother-in-law and a few stocking stuffers, but at least the Barbie Dream Mansion for his niece and the surprise he'd spent weeks planning for Mom and Dad were done deals. God knows his parents deserved something special after what they'd recently weathered. Mom's test results were expected this weekend—he prayed the news would be good and the dark cloud of worry that had hung over the entire family for these past weeks would disappear. He refused to consider any other alternative. Yup, this was going to be a great Christmas. Certainly better than last year...

"Sorry to keep you waiting." Debra's voice pulled him from his reverie. Her blue-eyed gaze glided over him in a slow, top to bottom ogle—an ogle he pretended not to notice. Probably he should have been flattered by her obvious interest, but in spite of the fact that Debra was attractive and smart, she didn't kindle the least reaction in him, which was just as well. Even if her flirtations had set him on fire, he wouldn't hesitate to douse those flames with a bucket of cold water. He'd learned the hard way not to fish off the company pier, and it was a lesson he had no intention of suffering through again.

"What can I do for you, Matt?" She pursed her full lips and gave him a look that clearly indicated she'd be happy to do anything he wanted.

He offered her an easy smile, making sure he was

merely polite and not overly friendly. "I need the number for the corporate travel agent."

"Sure." She flipped through her Rolodex, copied the information onto a sticky note, then handed it to him. "Several of us are going to Little Italy for dinner at Carmine's after work tonight." Her voice held suggestive undertones that made it sound more like they were going to a porn flick. "Would you like to...come?"

Oh boy. Keeping his expression bland, he shook his head. "Thanks, but I already have plans."

"A date?"

Probably he should say yes—*with my fiancée* and put an end to her interest, but he no longer had a fiancée, and he didn't like to lie. After having been the victim of painful lies, he hated being lied to—and that being the case, his conscience balked at telling untruths. Besides, his dad had always told him if you tell the truth, you don't have to remember what you've lied about.

"Thanks to a deadline, a date with my computer, working up some new ideas," he said.

She waggled a glossy-nailed finger at him. "You know what they say about all work and no play, Matt."

"Yup. That's me. A dull boy. Burning the midnight oil." Which was the gospel truth. Since today was Thursday, and he'd be leaving for Chateau Fontaine after work tomorrow, that didn't leave him much time to gather his thoughts and pull together a knockout presentation. He'd probably be pulling an all-nighter. Not that he had anything better to do. Ever since his breakup with Tricia last Christmas, his social life had flatlined. But that was okay by him. Work was a lot safer and a helluva lot less trouble than women.

A movement in his peripheral vision caught his eye and he turned, then barely suppressed a groan. Speaking of trouble and women, Jillian Taylor, the worst combination of those two things was heading down the hallway in his direction. As usual, her dark hair was pulled back into a severe, neat, reserved chignon. In fact, everything about her screamed severe, neat and reserved. Her hairstyle, her discreet makeup, her tailored suit.

Today she wore brown pin-striped, double-breasted, with slim pants and shoes that looked like high-heeled tassel loafers. A "don't mess with me" aura surrounded her like a force field. Thanks to his experience with Tricia, he recognized Jilly's type only too well—her reserved exterior hid a cold, competitive, ambitious interior. From his first day at Maxximum, he'd realized she could mess him up the same way Tricia had. From that moment on, he'd pegged Jilly Taylor as the one to beat. Public enemy number one.

Though he firmly kept himself out of the office gossip loop, he wasn't deaf, and on several occasions in the break room he'd heard male co-workers refer to Jilly as the Freeze Queen—a full rank up from the title of Ice Princess with which he'd mentally dubbed her. The few times he'd found himself wondering if her office nickname was directed at something more personal than her aloof demeanor, he'd banished the thought to the Siberia of his subconscious. What business was it of his whether or not she ever thawed that cool exterior? *Been there, done that, have the scars from the knife in my back to prove it.*

An image of Tricia flashed through his mind—Tricia with her sultry blue eyes, come-hither smile and promises of love. Annoyed that he'd allowed his former fiancée to enter his thoughts at all, he firmly pushed aside the memory, relieved that it now only brought irritation rather than the gut-twisting sense of betrayal it once had. But it was hard not to have thoughts of her sneak into his mind whenever Jilly Taylor was around, raising his "Danger Approaching!" radar, since Jilly and Tricia were so clearly cast from the same mold. Oh, they didn't look anything alike—Tricia was blond and petite and favored more feminine styles in contrast to Jilly's dark coloring and tailored suits. But they were both smart and talented—and very, very ambitious. Just the sort of co-worker who should come with a warning sign tattooed on their forehead.

He narrowed his eyes, watching Jilly pause to exchange a brief word with someone. Then she walked toward him once again, her head down as she studied the papers she held. Even from a distance, Matt could see that her lips were pursed in concentration, and that her brows were bunched in a frown. She walked with a brisk, no-nonsense stride, her black, slim rectangular-frame glasses perched on her nose.

Yes, she was the epitome of professional competence, and as much as he hated to admit it, she was immensely talented. She'd started working at the agency the year before him, and they were both on the fast track to promotion. *But after I land ARC, you'll be left in the dust, Jilly.*

Something that felt suspiciously like his conscience pricked him, but he firmly swatted the feeling aside. It was every man for himself in this business.

As Jillian neared Debra's desk, she glanced up from her papers. Her gaze zeroed in on him, and her steps slowed. Her expression remained coolly professional, but he'd caught that flash in her eyes, the one clearly indicating she wasn't thrilled to see him. He bit back a smile at that slight ruffling of her always-in-place feathers. Some perverse part of him enjoyed rocking her boat, though she had never lost her cool around him. What would it take to *really* break through that professional veneer and get her fired up and out of sorts?

He'd expected her to march right on by, but she surprised him by stopping. Matt inhaled and caught a whiff of the elusive scent he'd noticed the first time he'd sat next to her in the conference room. As always, Jillian Taylor smelled fresh and clean—like clothes that had dried outdoors in the spring sunshine. Since it was winter, it couldn't be her clothing that smelled that way. Must be something they used at her dry cleaners. Either that or the Ice Princess had discovered a fragrance called Clean Laundry, which he highly doubted.

"Debra, Matt," she murmured in a voice that somehow managed to sound both smooth and a bit husky, as though she'd just slipped from between silk bedsheets. She looked at him over the top edge of her glasses. "Nice job with the Heavenly Chocolate account. Very clever, fresh and hip."

He searched for a sign of insincerity in her expression or voice, but found none. Man, she was good. "Thank you. It was a 'sweet' deal."

Her lips didn't so much as twitch. "Of course, I would have given you a run for your money if I hadn't been laid low with the flu."

"I know you would have. But I still would have been the one to bring in the account."

"I'm sure you like to tell yourself that."

He smiled. "Well, I'm glad you're feeling better."

She smiled back. "I'm sure you like to tell yourself that as well. How are you doing on the Fabulous Feline Food account?"

"Fantastic. But you know me—I'm a creative magnet. I'm like catnip."

"Hmmm. I think I feel a hairball coming up." She

turned to Debra, effectively dismissing him as if she were the Queen of England and he a lowly footman. "Is Adam in?"

Debra nodded. "He's expecting you."

With a nod at both of them, she strode down the corridor, then knocked on Adam's door. Seconds later she disappeared into the office, closing the door behind her.

Matt's competitive and suspicious instincts kicked into gear. What sort of meeting were the two of them having?

"Well, now I understand," Debra said, pulling his attention back.

He looked at her, and the speculation gleaming in her eyes made him nervous. "Understand what?"

"Why you haven't picked up on any of the signals I've sent your way. Your receptors are all clogged up." Her gaze shifted pointedly toward the door where Jilly had just disappeared. "I saw those sparks between you."

An incredulous laugh escaped him. "You couldn't be more wrong."

She hiked a skeptical brow. "I know sparks when I see them."

"Well, if you saw sparks, they definitely weren't *those* kind of sparks. More like sparks of annoyance."

"Doesn't matter," Debra said, with a knowing gleam in her eye. "Any kind of sparks can start a fire."

AT SEVEN-THIRTY THAT EVENING, Jilly plopped down into a booth across from Kate Montgomery at their favorite Chinatown eatery for their standing Thursday night dinner "date," a weekly tradition since their college graduation six years earlier. Jilly slapped her hands on the Formica table and shot her best friend a broad grin. Kate worked at a law firm on Park Avenue and specialized in tax law. Jilly loved her in spite of the fact that she was gorgeous, brilliant and savvy. Indeed, clad in what Jilly suspected was most likely an Armani suit, her pale blond hair falling softly about her shoulders, Kate reminded Jilly of a young Grace Kelly.

"Looks like you had a good day," Kate remarked with an answering smile as Jilly slipped her overcoat from her shoulders.

"You have no idea. I have a chance to bring in a huge new client for Maxximum."

"Sounds exciting," Kate said, passing her a plastic-coated menu. "Who's the potential client?"

"ARC Software, to promote their new operating system that's going to be installed in all WellCraft computers." Adrenaline surged just saying the words.

Kate looked properly impressed. "That *is* huge. Landing something like that would cement your position at Maxximum."

"Exactly. There's a promotion, bonus and perks attached." Finally—the financial and career security she'd been striving for. "My boss, Adam, has arranged for me to spend time with ARC's CEO this weekend at—guess where?"

"Hmm...obviously somewhere good. Maui?"

Jilly laughed. "Not quite *that* good. Chateau Fontaine."

"Oohh. I'm green with envy. Ben and I spent a weekend there last summer and we loved it."

Jilly noted how Kate's eyes lit up when she mentioned her fiancé. "I'm hoping I'll have enough down time to squeeze in a facial."

"Oh, yeah, I'm feeling your pain," Kate said with dry humor. "I just *hate* it when I have to schmooze clients at Chateau Fontaine. When are you going?"

"Tomorrow after work. I won't be back until Monday night. As much as I hate to cut our 'date' short, I need to go home right after dinner. I only have tonight to prepare some sort of presentation. Doesn't give me much time to be brilliant.''

"That's fine. I have some briefs to go over for a meeting tomorrow.''

The waiter arrived, and they gave their selections—a no-brainer as they ordered the same thing every week.

"So, what else is going on?'' Kate asked. "How's your social life?''

"You mean besides my weekly date with you? Non-existent. What about you?'' Her gaze flicked down to the two-carat sparkler adorning Kate's left hand. "Judging from that neon glow emanating from you, things are going well with Ben.''

"Things are going *very* well with Ben. The wedding plans are progressing nicely. I highly recommend falling in love.''

"Of course you do. That's because you managed to find the last decent, honest, financially secure, emotionally stable, unmarried, heterosexual man in New York.''

"I *found* him because I was looking.''

"Actually, you weren't looking at all. As I recall, you were totally focused on your career.''

"I was only ninety percent focused on my career,'' Kate corrected, shifting into lawyer mode. "I kept ten percent of myself open to dating and searching for Mr. Right. Unlike you. You are one hundred percent work, one hundred percent of the time.''

"That's not true. I've jumped on the relationship band-wagon more times than I care to remember. And I've fallen off that wagon every time—with varying degrees of injuries.''

"Uh-huh. And when's the last time you took that leap?'' Kate asked, moving in for the kill.

"Okay, okay, it's been a while." Yeah, like nine months, three weeks and seventeen days. "But I can sum up my lack of interest in two words: Aaron Winston."

"That was months ago. And just because your last boyfriend turned out to have major control issues, doesn't mean that would happen with your next boyfriend."

"Sure, Aaron was the last one, but what about his predecessors Carl, Mike, Kevin, Rob...the list goes on. It seems as if *every* man I date has control issues. It's like I'm this big magnet—" she spread her arms to demonstrate "—that only attracts men who want to smother, change and control me. Well, that type and gay men. Unfortunately neither one works for me." When Kate appeared about to argue, Jilly plunged on, "Look, I'll admit I'm paranoid, but given my track record with men can you blame me?"

Kate heaved out a sigh. "I suppose not."

"Believe me, I'd love to have the sort of relationship that you share with Ben."

"And if the right guy came along...?"

"I'd grab him like *that.*" She snapped her fingers. "But I'm not holding my breath for Mr. Fabulous to walk by. And besides, I'm way too busy at work to spend time looking for this fictitious man."

"Excellent. That means you'll find him soon. The right guy always comes along when you're not looking."

"Sure. If you say so."

"I do. Believe me, when you least anticipate it, something unexpected will happen and—*poof!*—your world will be turned upside down."

Their waiter delivered their food, and having skipped lunch, Jilly immediately applied her chopsticks to her sautéed shrimp and broccoli.

"I wish there was someone at my office I could introduce you to," Kate said, filling their small, white, porcelain teacups with fragrant brew, "but they're all either married, gay, nearing retirement age or as mature as preschoolers."

"Hmmm. I thought all men fell into one of those categories."

Kate laughed. "Only ninety-nine percent. It's trying to find that elusive one percent that's the challenge. But Ben is proof that they're out there."

"Well, I don't have the time right now to devote to searching out the one remaining good apple in the barrel. Men require too much time and attention, both of which I'm currently out of." She shook her head. "Whoever said women were high maintenance was definitely a man. Where are all the guys I read about in *Cosmo* who like independent women who don't cling to them like vines? I certainly haven't met any." She stabbed a shrimp with the end of her chopstick. "Sure, they *say* that's what they want, but after a few dates, it seems as if guys develop expectations—like that I'll be at their beck and call, and that they can take charge of my life. Then they get testy if I need to cancel plans because of work."

"Amen, sister," Kate said. "The majority of men I met before Ben required nonstop ego stroking, and seemed to crave almost slavish devotion—not that they necessarily planned to return that slavish devotion, and not that I'd wanted them to, anyway—but they wanted it just the same."

"Yup. And the minute they realize my job is my top priority and I'm not willing to rearrange my entire schedule, or change my hair or fashion preferences or political beliefs or whatever to suit their every need, interest fizzles—on both sides. I don't want or need a man to take care of me, and I sure don't want a man who thinks he should be in charge all the time. I don't want the mess my mom found herself in to ever happen to me, which is why it's so scary that I almost fell into that trap with Aaron. I've worked too long and hard to make certain I can take care of myself—financially and emotionally."

"Oh, I agree," Kate said, popping a water chestnut into her mouth. "But—trust me on this—it's very nice to have someone else take care of you *physically* for a change."

Jilly shook her head at Kate's devilish grin. "You're killing me, you know that? Good grief, you practically have little bluebirds of happiness encircling your head like a wreath. If I didn't love you so much and weren't so happy for you, I'd have to bring you outside and slap the crap out of you for being so content and in love and sexually satisfied."

Kate laughed. "Well, maybe you'll meet the man of your dreams at Chateau Fontaine this weekend."

"Not likely. This is going to be strictly business."

"Just keep an open mind—in case Mr. Right happens to knock on your door." She raised her porcelain cup and fixed Jilly with a no-nonsense stare. "Promise?"

Jilly briefly looked toward the ceiling, but tapped the rim of her cup against Kate's. "All right, I promise. But the problem here is that because *you're* in love, you think *everyone* should be in love."

"Everyone should be," Kate agreed without hesitation. "Falling in love doesn't mean you're relinquishing all control or losing your independence." She reached out and squeezed Jilly's hand. "It doesn't have to be that way, Jilly. I used to think that, too—until I met Ben. There's a big difference between compromising your dreams and ambitions, and *sharing* them with someone. You'll understand when you meet the right guy."

Looking at Kate's earnest expression, at the happiness

that shone from her in almost visible rays, Jilly felt a pang of something resonate through her that she couldn't put a name to. Envy? Want? Probably. Who wouldn't want the sort of love Kate had with Ben?

"Well, until the right guy toddles along, my time and energy are focused on my career. And winning the ARC account would be a major coup."

"Speaking of which," Kate said, scooping more fried rice onto her plate, "I wonder what Matt Davidson will say when you land the account."

An odd tingle, no doubt indigestion brought on by the mention of Matt's name, fluttered through Jilly. "He'll probably claim in that infuriating, superior way of his that he could have landed the account in half the time, and with a better campaign. He thinks he's 'all that' because he brought in a big account while I was out with the flu. He's the most arrogant, ambitious, annoying, cut-throat,   doesn't-give-a-damn-about-anyone-but-himself person I've ever had the misfortune to meet."

Grrrr. The mere thought of Matt Davidson raised her hackles. He'd earned her enmity right from the beginning when he'd waltzed into Maxximum and promptly landed Strattford Furniture, an account she'd worked on for weeks. When she'd confronted him, demanding an explanation for stealing her account, he'd bristled, denying he'd ever do such a thing, claiming that Walter Stratt-ford was a long-standing friend of his family and had sought *him* out. After Matt's story had proven true, even though she was still irritated, Jilly had attempted to offer an olive branch, but clearly Matt wanted no part of her peace offering. He seemed to have singled her out as his main competition. As Jilly wasn't about to let him usurp her hard-won position at Maxximum, the line in the sand had been drawn.

Unfortunately, the part of her that demanded complete honesty had to admit—albeit grudgingly—that Matt Davidson's creative abilities were pretty impressive. Okay, incredibly impressive. And as if he wasn't already irritating enough, the guy had the nerve to be good-looking to boot. With his dark hair and deep blue eyes, Matt Davidson definitely wasn't hard to look at.

Still, she had no intention of turning her back on someone as openly ambitious as Matt. Advertising was dog eat dog, and she had no intention of getting devoured.

"Well, he might be your biggest rival and a pain in the butt," Kate said, yanking her from her reverie, "but based on that glimpse I caught of him that one time when you pointed him out, he's very cute."

"Yeah. Cute like a rattlesnake. You saw him at a distance. The closer you get, the less attractive he is, believe me." Her inner voice chanted something that sounded suspiciously like *liar, liar, pants on fire,* but she wrapped a muzzle on the pesky voice, and forced her annoying co-worker from her thoughts.

Her career was priority one. And with hard work and dedication, she had a feeling that this weekend at Chateau Fontaine was going to bring her everything she wanted.

2

STOPPING UNDER THE COLUMNED portico that stood in front of Chateau Fontaine's curved driveway, Matt shifted his Lexus into Park and gratefully exited the vehicle. His legs were stiff from six straight hours of sitting, and his ass felt like it weighed eight hundred pounds. For the amount of time he'd been in the car, he could have driven to damn Canada.

Of course, not arriving at Chateau Fontaine until the middle of the freakin' night was his own fault. What stroke of insanity had possessed him to attempt to *drive* out to the winery? He'd known there'd be traffic—hell, the Long Island Expressway wasn't called the World's Largest Parking Lot for nothing—but he'd figured that by not leaving the city until almost 8:00 p.m. he'd miss most of the congestion. Unfortunately he hadn't factored in the holiday shoppers on the road. Nor had he predicted the overturned tractor-trailer that had closed all eastbound lanes, clogging the roadway for miles. Or the snow that had started falling several hours ago.

After accepting a claim check from the valet and removing his black leather overnight bag from the trunk, Matt circled through the revolving glass door then crossed the cream marble floor, heading toward the registration desk as if it were an oasis in the desert. Damn, but he was tired. His eyes felt gritty, he was thirsty, and the energy provided by the Snickers bar he'd eaten at his desk for dinner was long gone. But at this point he was even too tired to eat.

"Hell, I'm even too tired for sex," he muttered. Now *there* was a sentence he didn't think he'd ever hear himself say.

All he wanted was to crawl into bed and pass out until his wake-up call. After pulling an all-nighter last night working up ideas for ARC Software, then suffering through a long, frustrating, headache-inducing day, topped off with the drive from hell, he was finished.

He'd wanted to check in early, to give himself a chance to relax and look over his notes before his breakfast meeting with Jack Witherspoon, but his crazy day had sunk those plans like a bowling ball tossed in a lake. He'd spoken to Jack this morning and since neither knew exactly what time they'd be arriving at the resort, they'd agreed it was best to meet first thing in the morning instead of tonight. Good thing, as Matt would have had to cancel.

When he arrived at the highly polished beige granite counter, he was greeted by a young woman whose name tag announced she was Maggie. Maggie appeared way too perky for the middle of the night.

Summoning a tired smile, Matt gave her his confirmation number by handing her the fax he'd received that morning from Maxximum's travel agent.

"Oh, yes, Mr. Davidson, you're all set," Maggie said with a friendly grin. She handed him a key card and a pamphlet. "This explains all our amenities. Take the elevators on your left to the third floor. Room 312 will be at the end of the hallway."

Room 312 sounded like Utopia, and the only amenity he needed right now was a bed. "I'd like to have a wake-up call, please, for six-thirty." That would give him plenty of time to relax and look over his notes before meeting with Jack Witherspoon at nine. He did his best thinking in the morning, and he was too exhausted to contemplate work now. What he needed now was sleep. He just hoped he'd find his bed before he passed out.

Nodding his thanks, Matt hoisted his overnight bag onto his shoulder and headed across the lobby, his tired gaze skimming over the lush, yet understated neoclassic decor. Christmas wreaths decorated with colorful glass ornaments hung on the walls, and long, fragrant boughs of pine draped the mantel. The entire back wall was glass and, he presumed, overlooked the vineyards. Vaulted ceilings, supported by marble columns wrapped in holiday twinkle lights, dotted the perimeter of the lobby. Lush foliage, planted in huge urns painted with scenes of pastoral vineyards, lent the room a gardenlike atmosphere. Thick rugs, their borders decorated with grapes, vines and leaves, were scattered around the room, as were plush, inviting chairs. An ivory grand piano stood majestically in the corner, near a curving staircase that led up to a loft area. There, a brightly lit Christmas tree glowed with jewel-tone lights.

He dozed off standing up in the elevator, awakening when his head bobbed forward with a sudden jerk as the car halted at the third floor and the doors slid open. Squinting his tired eyes against the bright light illuminating the hallway, he made his way down the leaf-patterned carpet to room 312.

After slipping the key card into the slot, he turned the brass handle when the green light flashed. He gratefully entered the room, closing the door behind him, and welcomed the soothing darkness after the irritatingly bright hallway light.

Bed, bed, bed his exhausted cells chanted. He plopped his overnight bag on the floor, then quickly removed his overcoat. Eyelids drooping, he toed off his dress shoes, then undressed with clumsy haste, tossing his clothing haphazardly over his bag, vowing to hang up everything in the morning when he could think straight. Stripped down to his boxer briefs, he stumbled in the dark toward the bed. With the small part of his brain that was still barely functioning, he noted the lumpy disarray of the covers on the far side of the bed. Humph. This might be a swanky resort, but the housekeeping left a lot to be desired. But who the hell cared? There was a pillow with his name on it only seconds away.

A long, satisfied sigh escaped him as he eased beneath the covers, and let his groggy head settle against the cushy pillow. The limp relaxation brought on by utter exhaustion closed in on him. Floating in a hazy state that bordered on just dropping off to sleep, he turned onto his side, and stretched out his arm.

His hand landed on something delightfully warm and silky. Satin sheets. A low hum of appreciation rumbled in his throat. Nice. His hand cruised upward, some deep recess of his fried brain vaguely appreciating the smooth texture. Soft. Smooth and curvy. Like a woman's breast.

His fingers gently kneaded the plump softness, and as sleep overcame him, his imagination conjured up a rosy nipple beading beneath his palm. He drew in a contented breath. *Oooooh,* baby. Yeah. This was some kind of fabulous bed. He shifted closer to the enticing softness, brushing his body against the delightful warmth. *Definitely gotta get me a bed like this....*

A low, throaty, sexy moan sounded, and the plump softness beneath his hand shifted. Warm breath touched his shoulder, and for one heavenly moment it felt as if feminine curves pressed against him. Before his brain could fully register the delightful sensation, a sharp gasp sounded next to his ear. What the—?

His eyeballs weren't even all the way open when he was pelted with a barrage of thrashing limbs and a slew of threats.

"Get away from me, you bastard," came a female voice filled with both fury and fright, "or I'll hand you your severed gonads on a platter."

Holy crap! That chased away all remnants of sleep like a bucket of ice water over the head, and he quickly cupped his privates.

The next instant light flooded the room, and he blinked against the sudden brightness. Looking up, he found himself staring at a vision of dark-haired fury. She stood on the mattress, chest heaving, eyes filled with a combination of fright and a lethal expression that made it clear his gonads were indeed in danger. She snatched up a paperback book from the nightstand and raised it above her head as if to hurl it at him. She looked like a one-woman kung fu, Swat team, fully prepared to kick his ass. "What the hell do you...?" Her furious question trailed off, and she narrowed her eyes. "Matt?"

Matt? She knew him? He uncupped himself and struggled to sit up. "Yeah. Who are...?" His struggling abruptly ended, and he stilled as a flash of disbelieving recognition hit him like a two-by-four to the head. He actually felt his eyeballs goggle. *"Jilly?"*

They stared at each other for several long seconds, silence stretching between them. Matt wasn't certain what was preventing her from speaking, but he sure as hell knew what had rendered *him* speechless.

The woman standing on the bed was most certainly Jilly Taylor, but except for the familiar facial features, nothing about this tousle-haired female resembled the Ice Princess.

Good God, this raven-haired temptress could ignite a bonfire in a rainstorm. Long, silky strands of midnight hair fell across her shoulders and down her back in tumbled disarray. Her golden-brown eyes, devoid of her rectangular glasses, appeared huge and startled. Crimson stained her cheeks, and her full lips were moist and parted.

Unlike the ultraconservative Jilly Taylor he knew, nothing about this woman screamed prim or proper. Smooth, creamy skin—a *lot* of it—was showcased by the black satin tank top she wore. His stupefied gaze skimmed over her delicate collarbone, focused on the way her chest rose and fell with her rapid breaths, then lowered to the swell of her breasts and the visible outline of her erect nipples pushing against the material. His fingers involuntarily clenched, vividly recalling the plump softness of what he now realized had been her breast filling his palm.

His gaze tracked lower still, over the several inches of flat, toned abdomen left bare between the end of her tank and the top of her low-rise black, lacy panties. And her legs...holy hell, the sight of those long, shapely bare legs nearly stopped his heart. She looked like she'd stepped off the pages of a Victoria's Secret catalog—right after a bout of hot sex.

Damn. No more need to wonder what was hiding under all those straitlaced suits she wore—not that he'd ever wondered, of course. But now he knew. And he knew not only what she looked like, but also what she felt like. Jilly possessed a warm, soft, womanly, fantasy-inducing body that was rapidly supplying a number of unwanted, ill-advised fantasies. Great. Just what he needed—a budding erection.

Forcing himself to concentrate on his annoyance rather than her nearly naked body, he cleared his throat—twice—to find his voice. "What are you doing here?"

She planted her hands on her hips and raised her brows, looking down on him from her vantage point like an avenging warrior. "Actually, I think the question is what are *you* doing here—besides breaking into my room and scaring me to death? Is this some kind of sick joke?"

Feeling at a distinct disadvantage sitting, he swung his legs over the side, stood, then returned her glare. "I don't play sick jokes. And what do you mean, *your* room? The girl at the registration desk gave me a key to room 312." Sudden doubt assailed him. "This *is* 312, isn't it?"

"Yes." She frowned. "There must be some mistake with the reservation." Her frown turned to a squinty-eyed, suspicion-filled glower. "But that doesn't explain what you're doing *here.* At Chateau Fontaine. Of course, one doesn't need to be a rocket scientist to figure it out. Listen, if you think you're going to weasel your way into my time with Jack Witherspoon—"

"Whoa! What do you mean *your* time with Wither-spoon?"

"Just that. Adam sent me out here to wine and dine Jack this weekend to convince him to hire Maxximum for his new ad campaign."

Matt narrowed his eyes and studied her closely. Either she was a remarkable liar, which was certainly possible, or Adam had sent both him *and* Jilly out here to woo Witherspoon, which unfortunately was also possible. "Is that so?" he said. "Well, Adam sent *me* out here to wine and dine Jack this weekend to convince him to hire Maxx-imum for his new ad campaign."

Still standing on the mattress, Jilly stared down at him for several long seconds, trying to gather her scattered wits. Her heart still slapped against her ribs—a result of two factors: one, fright at being awakened from a deep sleep to find herself no longer alone in bed, and, two, physical arousal from her sensual dream—of a warm, masculine hand caressing her breast, a hard, muscled body rubbing against hers—which had turned out not to be a dream at all. Jeez, it was a miracle she hadn't gone into cardiac arrest. If she hadn't hit the light switch and discovered it was Matt, she most likely would have croaked.

As for his explanation, could he possibly be telling the truth? Or had he found out about her travel plans and thought he'd try to win ARC's account for himself? Her suspicious gaze raked over him, which was a mistake, because her long sleeping libido suddenly woke up.

Whew. A veritable rainstorm of perfect genes had soaked this guy. She eyed his broad shoulders, and the smattering of dark chest hair that narrowed into a tantalizing ribbon, which bisected his six-pack abs before disappearing into white boxer briefs. Her gaze dipped lower, taking in his long, muscular legs, before wandering back up to rivet on his groin.

Double whew. She instantly recalled how warm and tingly and aroused she'd felt during those brief seconds she'd snuggled against him before she'd come fully awake. For some insane reason, Kate's words whispered through her mind. *When you least anticipate it, something unexpected will happen and—poof!—your world will be turned upside down.*

Good grief, she was losing her mind. Sure, this was unexpected, but in a very unpleasant way. Definitely not what Kate had meant at all.

"Well?" he asked, yanking her attention away from his way-too-fascinating crotch. Their eyes met, and awareness seemed to crackle between them. His watchful expression made it clear he was well aware he'd just received a thorough ogle. *Humph.* She certainly wouldn't feel embarrassed. After all, he'd ogled her first—surely a fact that should have annoyed her, rather than shoot heat through her veins. There'd been no mistaking his surprise—or his appreciation—when his gaze had roamed over her. It had been a long time since a man had looked at her as Matt just had. Of course, it had been a long time since she'd stood before a guy wearing next to nothing.

"Well, what?" she said, moving to step off the mattress and onto the floor.

He held out his hand to assist her, and without thinking she clasped his hand for balance. His long fingers wrapped around hers, rushing heat up her arm, igniting her nerve endings. The instant her feet were firmly planted on the carpet, she snatched her hand away as if he'd electrocuted her and backed several feet away from his disturbing presence. She felt raw and exposed, and she desperately wished she'd brought a robe. But all she had to cover herself with was her sweats, and they were in her overnight bag in the closet. Matt didn't seem disconcerted by their lack of clothing, and she wasn't about to give him the upper hand by allowing him to think she was uncomfortable.

You wear less to the beach, her inner voice rationalized. Yeah, she did. But skimpy lingerie had a whole different connotation than swimwear—especially in the confines of a bedroom, and with Matt Davidson around. Pushing aside her discomfort, she crossed her arms and raised her chin a notch.

"Well, I think it's pretty obvious what's going on

here," he said, his gaze fixed on hers, "assuming you're telling the truth about Adam sending you here—"

"I'm not a liar," she said through clenched teeth. "But perhaps *you* are."

"I'm a lot of things, but a liar isn't one of them."

"One phone call can verify that."

"Yes, it can." His gaze flicked to the digital clock on the nightstand which glowed 2:43 a.m. "Do you want to call Adam this late to ask him, or can you take my word for it until a more decent hour?"

She prided herself on reading people fairly well, and as much as she hated to admit it, Matt looked and sounded utterly sincere. If he was telling the truth...

Dread seeped slowly into her veins. "I'll give you the benefit of the doubt—until morning." She pushed her tangled hair off her face. "Besides, sending us both out here to woo the same client—while I don't want to believe Adam would do that to us again—"

"It looks like he's done it to us again." He blew out a breath. "Just like last summer, with the Lone Star Steak account. Pitting us against each other certainly insures that *one* of us will win the ARC account for Maxximum."

"Right. It worked with Lone Star, and clearly Adam hopes history will repeat itself. Smart tactic."

"One I would admire much more if I wasn't one of the victims." Matt muttered. "Again. And I don't intend to let history repeat itself."

"Meaning?"

"You won the Lone Star Steak account. I'm going to win this one."

She waved her hand in a dismissive gesture. "Yeah, yeah, yeah. Hey, whatever you need to believe to get you through the day. But your quest for ARC will be difficult to achieve when your weekend is spent explaining to the police why you broke into my room."

He shot her a glare. "I'm an ad exec, not a cat burglar. I told you. Registration gave me a key to 312 when I checked in." He moved to the phone resting on the pale oak desk in the corner. After consulting the directory listed on the phone's cream-colored surface, he lifted the receiver and punched in a number. "I'm calling the front desk to find out what's going on."

He turned his back to her and reached across the desk to slide a pad and pen closer to him. His underwear stretched across a taut male butt that deserved to be bronzed and displayed in the Smithsonian. Someone at the front desk must have picked up because Matt said, "Hello, Maggie. This is Matt Davidson..." He explained the situation, but Jilly only listened with half an ear as all her attention focused on the very distracting view of his backside.

This was not good. The sight of this guy in his Calvins was having an adverse affect on her ability to breathe straight and think right. Er, think straight and breathe right. Jeez, anybody would think she hadn't seen a gloriously masculine, almost naked man before. She had. Just not recently—unless one considered nine months, three weeks and eighteen days recent. And everything feminine in her that had lain dormant for those nine months, three weeks and eighteen days was suddenly bright-eyed and alert and *very* interested in this new masculine scenery.

Swell. Like she didn't have enough problems, now she had to go and develop a sudden case of the hots for her biggest rival. Why, oh why, did her body have to respond to *this* guy?

He hung up the phone, then turned to face her. "Did you catch all that?" he asked.

Heat crept up her neck. With her libido and hormones making so much racket, nothing he'd said had registered. "Er, not exactly. I was trying to, um, remember where I left my cell phone." Yup, that was her story and she was stickin' to it. "Why don't you summarize it for me?"

"You want the good news first or the bad news?"

"Good news."

"That's unfortunate because there is no good news. At least for you. The bad news is that only two rooms were booked for Maxximum Advertising."

"Right. One for you and one for me. So what's the problem?" Her bare foot tapped against the carpet.

"Noooo," he said in a voice one would use with a kindergartner. "One for Jack Witherspoon and one for me."

"*You?*" Anger propelled her forward until less than two feet separated them. At least her anger had shut down her hormones. More or less. Nothing was less attractive than an arrogant, infuriating man. Usually. Jamming her hands on her hips, she jutted out her chin. "In case it escaped your notice, you came into *my* room, where *I* was sleeping in *my* bed. *My* clothes are hanging in the closet, and *my* makeup and toothbrush are in the bathroom. That makes this *my* room. Possession is nine-tenths of the law." Reaching down, she yanked up the pile of masculine clothes draped over his luggage and slapped them against his bare chest. "So I suggest you get dressed and toddle on down to the registration desk, pick up a new key and stake your claim on a *vacant* room."

His lips curved into a smile that did not quite reach his eyes. "I'd be happy to, but that's where the rest of the bad news comes in. There are no more rooms available."

She looked toward the ceiling and prayed for patience. "Surely you don't expect me to believe that."

He shrugged. "Call the front desk. It's not that difficult to believe. There're only three dozen rooms here—this place is not exactly the size of a Hyatt."

Easing around him, she stalked to the phone and jabbed in the number for the front desk. A very pleasant young lady named Maggie regretfully confirmed that there were indeed no other rooms available, and no vacancies until the following Wednesday. At Jilly's request she checked the reservations. "A suite was booked at 8:20 yesterday morning for three nights for Maxximum Advertising by Surety Travel Agency."

"All right," Jilly said, nodding. That would be the suite Adam had booked for Jack Witherspoon. "What else?"

"A room was also booked for Maxximum yesterday," Maggie said, as Jilly heard computer keys tapping in the background. "That reservation came in at 9:53 a.m. by Surety Travel Agency, for a single room, for three nights."

"For just one room?"

"Yes, ma'am."

The bottom fell out of Jilly's stomach. One room. At 9:53. She thanked Maggie, then hung up. Turning to Matt, she asked, "When did Adam talk to you about the Witherspoon account?"

"Yesterday morning."

"What time?"

"Our meeting was at 9:30."

Oh boy. Her meeting with Adam had started at 9:45. Which meant that at 9:53, when the reservation was called in, she was still in Adam's office. Which meant that the travel agency had booked this room at *Matt's* request.

"Your meeting was after mine," he said, still clutching

his wrinkled clothes against his chest. Understanding dawned in his eyes. "I'm guessing this room was booked during the time you were meeting with Adam."

As much as she wanted to, there was no point in denying it. At least he had the decency not to look smug, which surprised her. "Obviously the travel agent made an error," she said. Yeah—like they'd neglected to book her damn room.

"Obviously."

"That's hardly my fault, Matt."

"Nor is it mine, Jilly."

"Well, I'm not leaving."

"Well, neither am I."

They stared at each other for several long, silent seconds, like two suspicious dogs circling each other, vying for the same bone. At this moment, the room was the bone. But, ultimately, Jack Witherspoon and the ARC Software account with all its accompanying perks was top prize. It was a huge career jump, winner take all, and Jilly had no intention of losing. Based on the stubborn set of Matt's features, neither did he.

She glanced toward the window and noted the heavy snow falling. Forcing him to leave, in the middle of the night, in the midst of a snowstorm seemed pretty inhumane. But she couldn't very well share the room with him. There was only one bed. And it wasn't even a king-size. No way was she lying in that not-king-size bed next to him and all that male pulchritude—again. Nope. No way. That scenario had disaster tattooed all over it. In Technicolor. Yet clearly the only way to get him out of this room would involve an atomic explosive, and she was fresh out.

"Look, Matt, surely there must be a sofa or roll-away bed somewhere at the resort you can sleep on."

He lifted a brow. "I asked, and according to Maggie, there are no roll-aways available. As for a sofa, I guess there're some in the lobby, but I'm not about to sleep there—especially not when there's a perfectly comfortable bed right here."

"A bed that's already occupied."

"It's big enough for two."

She opened her mouth to protest, but before she could utter a sound, he continued, "Don't worry, I'm not one of those guys who thrash around. Hell, I don't even snore. Do you?"

"No, but—"

"Great. Not that it would matter much. I'm so exhausted, even if you sawed wood like a lumberjack it wouldn't keep me awake. Look, there's not much we can do about this mess now, so let's just get some sleep. Maybe we can get the room problem sorted out in the morning." He yawned hugely, then plopped his clothes back down onto the top of his luggage. The sight of all that lovely male bareness momentarily robbed her of speech, and she could only watch as he bent down and pulled a brown leather shaving kit from the side pocket of his overnight bag. He entered the bathroom, closing the door behind him with a decisive click. Seconds later she heard water running.

"What are you doing?" she called.

"Brushing my teeth."

He emerged a minute later, and walked past her, leaving her to breathe in a whiff of his masculine scent mixed with mint. After pulling back the covers on the far side of the bed, he scrunched up the pillow, then laid down on his side facing away from her.

"'Night, Jilly. Sweet dreams."

'Night, Jilly? Sweet dreams? Was he insane? He didn't

look insane, but what did she know? There had to be *some* inkling of insanity lurking under that masculine exterior if he thought there was a snowball's chance in hell of her being able to *sleep* next to him. And dream? Not likely. No, she'd stare up at the ceiling, listening to him breathe, remembering what he'd felt like pressed up against her, cupping her breast, hating herself for remembering, and growing more and more annoyed that her presence obviously had no effect on him.

This was what came of concentrating too much on her career and not devoting enough attention to her social life. Nine months, three weeks and eighteen days of celibacy, mixed with a nearly naked gorgeous man was proving disastrous to her ability to keep her wits about her. And this with a guy she didn't trust as far as she could throw him. Thank God she didn't like him or else this situation would be a *real* disaster.

She gazed down at him, noting that his breathing was already slow and regular. Since she'd made it a rule long ago to steadfastly avoid any activities that could result in jail time, there was no point in contemplating tossing him over the balcony. Besides, based on the heated shivers she'd already experienced, touching him was *not* a good idea.

She eyed the chintz-covered wing chair near the desk, but decided it was ridiculous to attempt to sleep on it. All that would result in would be a stiff neck, and why should she? This was *her* room! Maybe it had been booked at his request, but she'd gotten here first. Squatter's rights, and all that. And Matt, drat him, was already asleep. If he could live with these arrangements for the next few hours, so could she.

Switching off the light, she gingerly slid between the covers. Moving as little as possible, she situated herself on her side as close to the edge of the mattress as possible without falling off, facing away from Matt. Once she was comfortable, she blew out a long breath of relief.

There. This wasn't so bad. So what if his beautiful, barely covered body rested less than three feet away? So what if she could hear him breathing? What difference did it make that she could feel the heat emanating off him against her back? Why, she barely noticed.

Yeah right, her inner voice snickered. *That's why your heart is pounding, your nipples are hard, and your body feels like it's roasting over a slow flame.*

Humph. Why the heck couldn't she be like Matt? He wasn't having any trouble sleeping, a fact which irked her to no end, driving sleep even further away.

She squeezed her eyes shut and prayed for sleep, strongly suspecting that that was one prayer destined to go unanswered.

MATT LAY IN THE DARK, wide-awake, forcing slow, even breaths into his lungs, but the effort cost him as he was decidedly short-winded, as if he'd run a mile uphill. Instead of falling into the dead sleep that had beckoned less than an hour ago, he felt like someone had hooked him up to a nuclear power plant and flipped the switch. Where the hell had his gritty-eyed, muscle-weakening exhaustion disappeared to?

Stupid question. He knew where it had gone—straight out the window the instant he'd clapped his bugged-out eyeballs on a nearly naked Jilly Taylor. An hour ago he'd thought he was too tired for sex. Ha! Now he couldn't erase the thought from his overactive mind, not to mention his very alert body.

How was a guy supposed to sleep when all that warm, smooth, fragrant, silky, bare female flesh was within reach? Flesh that he'd touched. Molded beneath his hand. Feminine softness that had pressed against him. Damn it, he wanted to touch her again. This time while fully awake.

Why the hell didn't her sleepwear match the sort of clothes she wore to work? Instead of black satin, she should have been wrapped up, chin to toes, in flannel.

Of course, all those carbs and sugar in the candy he'd consumed for dinner wasn't helping the situation. He brightened immediately. Yeah, that's why he couldn't sleep—carbs and sugar. And this slight arousal problem? Just an involuntary body response.

Slight *arousal problem?* his inner voice scoffed. *Right. And Jilly Taylor almost naked is just slightly gorgeous. And the knowledge that she's less than an arm's length away is only slightly disturbing.*

He heard her sigh and his every muscle tensed. This was *not* good.

And this was going to be one hell of a long night.

3

A PERSISTENT RINGING PENETRATED Matt's brain. He pried open one eyeball and groaned. Darkness. Who the hell was calling him in the middle of the night?

He reached out and snatched up the receiver. Before he could say a word, a perky mechanical voice said, "Good morning, this is the wake-up call you requested. The time is 6:30 a.m. Have a good day."

His eyes flew open. Wake-up call. Chateau Fontaine. Jack Witherspoon.

Jilly Taylor.

He sat up like someone had attached a catapult to his shoulders. Turning, he noted with relief that his sleep-destroying co-worker was not in the bed with him. Raking his hands through his hair, he registered the sound of the shower running.

Instantly, an image of Jilly, wet, naked and soapy filled his mind, and his groin instantly tightened. Terrific. A morning erection. This day was only forty seconds old and already it sucked. Frowning, he shook his head to clear away the lust-filled fog she'd somehow enveloped him in. What on earth was wrong with him? Hunger. Lack of sleep. Obviously he'd dozed off at some point during the wee hours, but he felt anything but rested. He needed coffee, and lots of it. He wondered if room service would provide him with a caffeine IV drip.

Swinging his legs over the edge of the mattress, he

stood and rolled his shoulders to loosen his tense muscles, then walked to the window. A peek through the pale green curtains revealed that it was still dark, the expanse of flat landscape illuminated only by the resort's floodlights. Fat snowflakes continued to fall, blanketing the outdoors with a carpet of white.

The shower cut off, and he turned, quickly crossing to his overnight bag where he pawed through his clothes, then pulled out a pair of dark blue sweatpants. He'd just slipped them on when the bathroom door opened, engulfing him in a cloud of fragrant steam. A tousle-haired, damp, towel-clad Jilly Taylor materialized from that lusciously scented vapor, a curvaceous goddess emerging through the mist like Venus gliding to the shore in a Botticelli painting.

She caught sight of him and stopped dead in her tracks, clutching the sarong-wrapped towel tighter against her breasts. Every thought except *Whoaaaaa, baby* fled from his head.

It certainly wasn't the best moment for him to forget how to speak English, but unfortunately God had given him a brain and a penis, and only enough blood for one of them to function at a time. And at this particular moment, his brain was not in charge. And when—make that *if*—his brain was ever in charge again, he was going to try to recall when he'd last been so powerfully attracted to a woman.

"I didn't know you were up," she said.

You don't know the half of it. Reaching down, he snatched up his sweatshirt from his overnight bag which yawned open at his feet. He rose and, feeling like an idiot, held the worn, gray material in front of his crotch in what he hoped was a nonchalant way. "I left a wake-up call. I'm meeting Jack for breakfast at nine."

Something flashed in her eyes, sending up a warning flag. Narrowing his eyes, he asked, "What time are you meeting with him today?"

She hesitated, then said, "I'm having breakfast with him as well. At seven-thirty."

Matt's fingers tightened around his sweatshirt. The fact that she was meeting with Jack first didn't bode well. Damn it, she'd have her foot in the door first, a definite advantage. But the real question was, how far would Jilly go to win ARC'S account? She was ambitious—was she unethical as well? On a clean playing field, he could compete with anyone. But would she play fair? Or would she turn out to be another Tricia and use her feminine wiles to win Jack's favor? After their breakup, he'd learned Tricia had slept with a potential client to get his business. Would Jilly do the same? If so, that was definitely something he couldn't compete with, and gave her an advantage that set his teeth on edge.

"Look, Matt, I've been thinking a lot about this," she said, regaining his attention. "I'm not any happier about our situation than you are. I think Adam placed us both in a very awkward situation, made even worse by the fact that we're going to end up sharing this room. I called the front desk when I woke up, and there's nothing they can do. And I don't see either one of us checking out and finding a room elsewhere...right?"

"*I'm* not moving out."

"Right. And neither am I." She pushed her damp hair back, tucking the dark strands behind her ear, and he absolutely did not notice how smooth and silky and touchable her damp flesh appeared. "That being the case, I think we should lay some ground rules—just a few guidelines to keep the level of awkwardness down to a minimum."

"What did you have in mind?"

"Well, first, I think we should agree to remain, um, clothed at all times."

Her gaze skimmed over his bare chest, and he wasn't sure if he was more relieved or alarmed by the quick flash of unmistakable desire he saw flicker in her eyes. Relieved, because, thank God he wasn't the only one feeling this unwanted attraction. By damn, misery loved company. But alarmed, because, holy hell, if she was feeling the same powerful desire he was, how could they possibly hope to fight it?

He nodded slowly, forcing his gaze to remain on hers and not wander over her luscious form. "Fine. Clothes on at all times. Although, I have to warn you, that's going to make showering a challenge."

Her lips twitched, drawing his attention to their ripe fullness. How was it possible that he'd worked with her all these months yet neglected to notice how beautiful her mouth was? He made a mental note to schedule an appointment to have his eyes checked. Or maybe he had noticed, but since he hadn't been thinking about Jilly in terms of kissing her, the lusciousness of her mouth just hadn't registered.

Well, it was registering now. Big time. Those full, pouty, unpainted lips silently beckoned him to step forward and taste them. It was all he could do to keep his bare feet planted in place and not give in to the temptation.

"Clothes on at all times—except to shower," she amended.

He nodded his agreement. "What else?"

"Well, in the interest of fair play, I think we should agree to stay out of each other's way as far as Jack Witherspoon is concerned." Her golden-brown gaze was direct and steady. "I want this account. I intend to play hard, and I always play to win. I fully expect the same from you. But it's not my style to play dirty. I'd like the same consideration from you."

He studied her for several seconds, trying to figure out what her angle was. Sure, she *seemed* honest, *sounded* trustworthy, *looked* sexy—er, sincere, but he wasn't about to be taken in again by an ambitious competitor. "You mean don't encroach on each other's time with Jack?" he asked.

"Exactly. Or try to sabotage each other's work."

He raised a brow, irked and insulted by the suggestion. "You don't have a very high opinion of me, do you?"

"I'm suspicious by nature."

"As am I."

"Which is why I think it's important that we lay these ground rules. I have every intention of fighting, but you have my word that I'll fight fair—provided you promise you'll do the same."

"Contrary to what you obviously believe, I don't cheat," he said, unable to keep the edge from his voice. "I don't need to."

"Good. Neither do I." She held out her hand. "Deal?"

Although he remained suspicious of her motives, he nodded. He'd play as fair as she did. So long as she kept up her end of the bargain, so would he. But if she played the seduction card with Jack, all-out war would rage, and then she'd be sorry. *All's fair in love and war, Jilly.* Not that love had anything to do with this. No. Just war. And he hoped it wouldn't come to that.

He clasped her hand. Her handshake was firm and professional, and the brief contact certainly shouldn't have whooshed heat up his arm. He had to fight back the urge to yank her into his embrace and start off the morning by breaking the rule of keeping clothes on at all times. Her skin felt so warm and soft against his fingers, and she was only wearing that skimpy towel...

He gave himself a firm mental shake. He needed to remember who and what she was—an ambitious co-worker. A rival who wanted nothing more than to pull the ARC account out from underneath him. Of course, that'd be much easier to recall once she put on some damn clothes. As soon as she was once again dressed in one of her conservative, don't-mess-with-me suits, and had her hair all pulled back in that severe bun, all would realign in his universe. Then he'd be able to shake her hand and not feel a thing.

His gaze slid over her, and he stifled a groan. Man, even when she was again fully clothed, it was going to be really, *really* difficult to erase from his mind the sensual image of Jilly Taylor fresh from the shower. But he could do it. He'd accomplished tougher quests, completed more difficult missions. He was up to the task.

She stepped back and gave him a slightly shaky smile. "I'll just get my makeup bag, then the bathroom's all yours."

"Uh, thanks."

She emerged from the bathroom seconds later, a tan leather pouch clutched to her midsection. He watched her walk past him, his gaze attached to her backside as if velcroed there, his imagination conjuring up the very fine sight he knew lurked beneath that towel. His erection stirred against his sweats and, with a frown, he stomped into the bathroom and closed the door with a decisive click.

He tossed his sweatshirt onto the white marble counter

and looked down at his tented sweatpants and grimaced. Damn. Had he just thought he was *up* to the task?

Well, it certainly appeared that he was.

Damn, damn, double damn.

JILLY LISTENED TO THE BATHROOM door close behind Matt, then squeezed her eyes shut and blew out a long, fervent sigh of relief.

When she opened her eyes, her gaze fell on the rumpled bed where they'd slept. Together. A humorless sound escaped her. Slept? Ha! Good thing she'd caught some z's before he'd arrived because she hadn't slept a wink the rest of the night. All she could think about was the warm, sexy, almost-naked male body less than three feet away. She'd recalled what that body felt like pressed against her. Wondered what it would look like completely naked...and feel like wrapped around her. Her very unruly hormones were letting her know in no uncertain terms that nine months, three weeks and now nineteen days were their absolute limit.

When the digital clock had finally glowed 6:00 a.m., she'd risen and indulged in a long, steamy shower in an effort to wash the image of Matt Davidson from her mind. Instead, all she'd accomplished was stirring up a maelstrom of fantasies in which she, Matt, the pulsating shower, and a bar of soap figured prominently. Disgusted with herself and this uncharacteristic, unwanted and unacceptable lust, she'd finally managed to set her sensual thoughts on the back burner long enough to formulate a set of ground rules to present to Matt—rules she'd arrived at purely for the purpose of self-preservation. While she had no intention of roaming around undressed in front of him, she wasn't certain how uninhibited he might be regarding nudity, and she absolutely, positively, did *not* want to see him naked.

Yeah, right, her detestably honest inner voice chimed in. *You want to see him naked more than you want to be able to eat unlimited Rocky Road ice cream and not have it permanently adhere to your ass.*

Yikes. Since that Rocky Road fantasy was one of her fondest dreams, this was not good. Okay, so she wanted to see him naked. Big deal. Who wouldn't? She was female and possessed a healthy, if somewhat recently starved, libido. But damn, why did it have to be *him* who had her insides melting to goo? This was like sleeping with the enemy. She glanced again at the rumpled bed, eyeing his still scrunched-up pillow that rested perilously close to hers. This *was* sleeping with the enemy.

Well, she just needed to remember that that's what he was. The enemy. The only thing standing between her and bringing home the ARC account. She could well imagine that he intended to try to turn this weekend into a "boys' club" scotch-swilling, cigar-smoking bonding session with Jack Witherspoon. Probably planned to hang out in the men's locker room, and take a steam—or whatever the hell men did in locker rooms. She couldn't compete with that. And she wouldn't let him get away with it, either.

Drawing a resolute breath, she marched over to the closet and mulled over her wardrobe possibilities, finally deciding on her red suit. The color was bright and empowering, and its slim skirt that hit just above her knees provided the perfect combination of professionalism and femininity. As soon as she was dressed, she'd feel more in control. All this bare skin was too distracting. What she needed was a robe—a heavy-duty one—and she made a mental note to visit the gift shop to see if they

sold any. In the meanwhile, it was time to forget about
Matt and focus her attention on Jack Witherspoon and
the ARC account. Fortunately, with her strong work
ethic, she knew she'd be able to focus on winning the account. Unfortunately, with everything female in her raising a ruckus, she wasn't so sure she'd be able to forget
about Matt Davidson.

MATT TURNED THE BRASS knobs to shut off the shower,
then reached for one of the thick, white towels. Securing
the terry cloth around his waist, he blew out a long
breath. The pulsating hot water had refreshed him,
cleaned the cobwebs from his brain, and—thankfully—
washed his ardor down the drain.

The muffled hum of a hair dryer filtered through the
door, indicating Jilly hadn't left yet. No problem. He'd
just shave and brush his teeth, and surely by that time
she'd be on her way out. Then he'd order up some coffee
from room service and go over his presentation for Jack.

Whistling softly under his breath, he wiped off a sec-
tion of the steamy mirror then pulled his razor from his
shaving kit. He'd just finished applying a thick layer of
shaving cream to his face and throat when a knock
sounded on the door.

"Matt? I'm sorry to bother you, but are you going to be
much longer in there?"

His body tensed at the mere sound of her voice. Damn.
"I'm just about to shave. Why?"

"Well, I'm ready to go, but I need to brush my teeth. I
can stand the sight of your razor blade if you can stand
the sight of my toothbrush. How about sharing the
sink?"

He hesitated, then glared at himself in the mirror. *Get a
hold of yourself, man. It's not as if you've never shared bath-*

room space with a woman before. Be cool, be casual, and let her *be the one thrown off balance.*

Drawing a resolute breath, he opened the door. "Sure, come on...in."

His words faltered as he took in her appearance. His gaze traveled over her, his brain noting that her fire-engine red suit was tasteful, flattering, and conservative. All his nerve endings, however, noted that it hugged her curves and showcased her legs in a way that made him feel as if someone had set a match to his towel.

His wayward gaze jumped upward. Their eyes met, and his jaw clenched at the unmistakable awareness simmering in her golden-brown depths. Then he noted the dark, silky curtain brushing her shoulders. "Your hair is down," he said in a voice ripe with suspicion.

She raised her brows and looked at him as if he'd just escaped from a mental ward. "What are you—the hair police? Listen, unbound hair may possibly be illegal in certain parts of the world, but here's a news flash—New York isn't one of them."

"You always wear your hair pulled back." He should have known better than to trust her. Here she was already breaking their "play fair" rule. He didn't doubt for a minute that this new look, which was decidedly softer and sexier than her usual severe hairstyle, was an attempt to use her feminine charms to sway Jack Witherspoon. The question was, exactly how many of her feminine charms would she be willing to use to win the account?

"I don't *always* wear it pulled back. Some days, like today, I just happen to have a good hair day."

Good hair day? She could say that again. Those thick, glossy raven curls had him fisting his hands to ward off the overwhelming urge to sift his fingers through them.

"And before you cast aspersions on anyone else's coif," she said, her eyes alight with amusement, "you might want to check your own. You've got a kind of 'finger-in-the-light socket' look happening right now—" her gaze roamed over his shaving cream-covered face and her lips twitched "—Santa."

Annoyance snaked through him. "That's from towel-drying. Not primping."

She blinked, then laughed. "Primping? *Me?* You've got to be kidding. I'm about as low maintenance as you can get. Since we're forced to share space this weekend, you'll be relieved to know I don't take an hour in the bathroom. I do, however, require a minute or two to brush my teeth, which is what I'd like to do now—if you don't mind?"

Decidedly irritated, but not certain if the feeling was directed more at her or at himself, Matt stepped back, out of the doorway, and she breezed in, her shiny black, high-heeled pumps clicking against the white ceramic tile floor. He breathed in and his senses were inundated with the delicate fresh scent of clean laundry.

"Thanks," she said, reaching for the toothpaste and toothbrush resting in a water glass in the corner. He tried to busy himself with his razor, but found himself immobile as the intimacy of them sharing this small space hit him like a punch in the gut. The sight of her bent over the sink sent his heart into overdrive, and he had to draw a deep, steadying breath—which didn't help at all since it only served to fill his head with her elusive fragrance.

Before he roused himself from his stupor, her toothbrush landed back in the glass with a soft *clink,* and she patted her mouth dry with the corner of a hand towel. Without so much as glancing at him, she tossed out a breezy "thanks," then exited the bathroom. Seconds later she reappeared in the doorway, clutching the handles of a black leather laptop case.

"I'm leaving," she said. "I guess I'll see you later."

"I guess so."

She hesitated, then said, "In the spirit of fair competition, especially as this is the holiday season, I wish you luck. May the best man win."

"Right back at you, Jilly."

She left the room, the door closing behind her with a muted click. He narrowed his eyes at that closed door. Fair competition? We'll see, Miss Wearing My Hair Down. But no matter what, Matt intended to see that the best *man* did indeed win the ARC account.

"HEY, HONEY—WHAT'S TAKIN'" so long to get a refill? Let's get on the stick." Jack Witherspoon's impatient voice cut across the dining room as he raised his empty coffee cup and shot the waitress a glare. He then returned his attention to Jilly and shook his head. "Cripes, I get better service at the diner. For the airs this place puts on, you'd think they could hire some decent help. At least someone smart enough to keep the coffee coming. How hard is that?"

Jilly bit the inside of her cheeks to hold back the reply that trembled on her lips. Everything in her longed to tell Jack to be fruitful and multiply—but not exactly in those words. As embarrassing and rude as she found his behavior, it certainly wouldn't endear her to him to point out that most people did not slug back a full cup of coffee every twelve seconds and that to keep his coffee cup filled would require the waitress to remain standing next to their table.

And he probably wouldn't appreciate a reminder that this was a restaurant, not a pig trough, although his table manners indicated that he wasn't aware of the distinction.

The waitress approached, bearing an ornate silver coffeepot. As she refilled Jack's cup, she said, "I'm sorry, sir. We were brewing a fresh pot."

"Well, leave this one right here and go brew another one. I don't feel like waiting 'til lunchtime to get another cup."

Color suffused the young woman's face, and she pressed her lips together as she walked away, no doubt to keep from telling Jack to go to hell, which is what Jilly wanted to do—right after she slapped him upside his rude head. Treating restaurant servers like dirt was one of her hot buttons. She'd worked in a pub during college, and her mom still waitressed at the same restaurant where she'd worked for the past twelve years, ever since Jilly's dad had died.

She swallowed her anger and kept her professional mask firmly in place. She wasn't quite sure what she'd expected from Jack Witherspoon, but it seemed that a man in his mid-fifties who'd risen to the level of prominence that he had would have more class. And manners. Yet, she'd successfully dealt with many clients she hadn't particularly liked. The trick was to keep things strictly business and not let her personal feelings and preferences muddy the waters. Like her personal feelings that Jack Witherspoon was an ass and that she wanted to pop him in the eye. Hmmm. That made him the second person in the last six hours she wanted to do that to. The other one being a certain co-worker who was currently her roommate. An image of Matt instantly popped into her mind. Matt undressed, wearing only a towel...

"So tell me about the ideas you've worked up for me, Jilly," Jack Witherspoon said, leaning back in his chair and stirring a spoonful of sugar into what had to be his eighth cup of coffee.

At last. Blinking away the distracting image of her unwanted roommate, she adjusted her glasses and began, "The biggest complaint consumers have about the current operating systems on the market is that they're undressed."

Jack raised a brow. "Undressed?"

"Er, I meant unstable. *Unstable.*" She cleared her throat. "Therefore, we'll emphasize your Lazer System's biggest selling point—no crashing. Also, the sophisticated defense mechanism that limits data damage due to viruses will enthuse many buyers." She reached down into her black leather case and pulled out her laptop and a manila folder, setting them both on the table.

Once she'd opened the laptop, she turned it on. "I've prepared a brief PowerPoint presentation to give you an idea of the concept I've worked up for Lazer." Her fingers flew across the keyboard, then she turned the screen so he could see the slide-show presentation she'd prepared.

"We'll plan a full media blitz. Go nationwide with radio spots on all the highest Arbitron rated stations in major cities. Full-page black-and-white ads in all the major newspapers and journals, and full-page, four-color ads in the top twenty magazines. Thirty-second television spots to air during prime time on all the major networks." She tapped the touch pad and the image of the logo and slogan she'd drawn up appeared. "Lazer. Precision in computing. Accuracy in results. It doesn't get any better."

Another image of Matt instantly flashed in her brain. Matt, about to drop his pants, a sexy smile on his face, saying in a husky, suggestive voice, *It doesn't get any better.*

Heat flooded her cheeks and she blinked rapidly to dispel the distracting image. When the slide-show ended, she passed Jack the folder with hands that weren't quite steady. "I...I've worked up some preliminary cost figures along with a revenue analysis, as well as a time frame for the ad placements for six- twelve- and eighteen-month periods."

He pulled a pair of reading glasses from his shirt pocket and slid them onto his nose. He fired out a barrage of questions and seemed to approve of her answers, which thankfully, didn't include the word "undressed." Based on the questions he asked, it was obvious that, though he might be lacking in the tact and manners department, he was razor-sharp when it came to business.

While he studied her revenue and market share projections, she took the opportunity to lean back in her chair, draw a much needed cleansing breath and cast a surreptitious glance at her watch. Eight thirty-five. Excellent. She still had a good twenty minutes to wrap things up before Matt appeared.

Since Jack was still engrossed, she looked around the tastefully decorated dining room, her gaze panning over the cream walls, the brass sconces, and the enormous marble fireplace where a cheery fire burned, lending an air of warmth and coziness to the room. She noted the framed paintings dotting the wall, all depicting pastoral vineyard scenes. A row of windows overlooking the snow-covered winery. An antique cherry sideboard. A glass-front cabinet filled with an array of colorful wine bottles. A brightly lit Christmas tree in the corner. Guests enjoying their breakfast.

Matt Davidson watching her from the table directly behind Jack.

When their eyes met, he lifted his coffee cup in salute with one hand and gave her a thumbs-up with the other.

Anger arrowed through her and she pressed her lips together. Damn it, how long had he been sitting there? If it was more than fifteen minutes, from his vantage point he would have witnessed her entire PowerPoint presentation, not to mention her verbal blunder. So much for their truce. It certainly hadn't take him long to slip into spy mode. She gave herself a hard mental slap for thinking, for even half a second, that someone as ambitious as Matt could be trusted.

Well, this was good. She was glad. She'd needed this wake-up call to prove to her pulsating hormones and traitorous body that, yeah, okay, she really did need to get out and have a social life—and Matt was definitely not the guy to contemplate being social with.

Without giving him the satisfaction of shooting him the "you're scum" glare he so richly deserved, she returned her attention to Jack. He glanced up at her, then slipped off his reading glasses.

"This is very impressive, Jilly. I like your ideas, and the ads you designed are eye-catching and unique. Just the sort of concept I want for Lazer."

She smiled. "I'm glad you like them. Naturally I'd be happy to rework anything you feel needs tweaking."

"Great." He closed the folder, then consulted his watch. "Since you and Matt Davidson are both with Maxximum, I guess you know I'm meeting him at nine."

She somehow resisted the urge to wrinkle her nose. "Yes."

"That boss of yours," Jack said with a chuckle, shaking his head, "Adam Terrell, is quite the sly fox, sending you both out here this weekend."

Jilly could easily think of half a dozen things other than

sly fox she'd like to call Adam Terrell right now. "Well, you know Adam," she said, praying her smile didn't appear as forced as it felt.

He glanced again at his watch. "Unless there's something else, I'd like to head back up to my room before I meet with Matt. Couple of phone calls I need to make."

"Of course." She closed up her laptop. "I thought you might enjoy a private tour of the winery followed by a wine tasting this afternoon. Is three o'clock convenient for you?"

"Sounds good. I'm having a massage at one, so that works out fine."

"Then I'll meet you in the lobby at three."

He nodded, then left the dining room, never looking in Matt's direction. The instant Jack was out of sight, Jilly pushed back her chair. Before she could rise, Matt slipped into the chair Jack had just vacated.

"Very nice presentation," he said, the chilly edge in his voice matching the ice in his glare.

She flicked her gaze over him as if he were something she'd just scraped off the bottom of her shoe. "Well, I guess you would know, seeing as how you saw fit to spy during my time with Jack."

"I wasn't spying. I was drinking coffee. It's hardly my fault that there aren't soundproof barriers and six-foot walls between the tables here."

"You could have had your coffee in the Bistro, or the bar, or you could have called room service. I should have known better than to trust you."

"Right back at ya, kiddo."

"What does that mean?"

"Why don't you just throw me over your shoulder and burp me, 'cause you obviously think I was born yesterday." His gaze wandered over her from head to toe, then he leaned forward until his face was a mere foot away from hers. There was no mistaking the anger simmering in his dark blue eyes. "Don't think I don't know what you're doing with your sexy skirt and sexy shoes and sexy hair." His gaze settled for several seconds on her mouth. "And sexy red lips."

Jilly stared at him, outrage pumping through her veins. "Not that I owe you any explanations," she said in a low voice that throbbed with anger, "but you should know that just because the 'casting couch' is alive and well in advertising, doesn't mean that everyone lies down on it. I told you I don't play dirty and I meant it. Unfortunately for me, you obviously can't say the same. Just don't judge other people by your own lack of standards. When I'm on the job, I conduct myself in a professional manner, in both my dress and my conduct. Always." She stood, then looked down at him with a scathing glare. "If you think my skirt and shoes and hair and red lips are sexy, then that's *your* problem."

Picking up her laptop, she turned, and without a backward glance, walked swiftly from the dining room.

Matt stared after her, an uncomfortable feeling invading his chest. A feeling he didn't like one bit. A feeling that suggested he'd just made a big mistake. There was no doubt she was pissed off. Was her outrage genuine, or an act? It certainly seemed real, but if she planned to seduce Jack Witherspoon, she certainly wouldn't admit it. His suspicions lingered, but in all fairness he had to admit there was nothing blatantly sensual about her attire.

If you think my skirt and shoes and hair and red lips are sexy, then that's your problem.

Yeah, well, he *did* think they were sexy. Sexy as hell. And *that* definitely was a problem.

The question was, what did he intend to do about it?

4

JILLY STEAMED INTO ROOM 312, annoyed at Matt Davidson, but even more annoyed at herself. After pushing the
door closed with a hard hip-check, she kicked off her
shoes, set her laptop on the dresser, then plopped onto
her back on the freshly made bed, her stockinged feet
hanging over the edge of the forest-green, grapevine-
embroidered comforter.

What on earth was wrong with her? Never before had
her mind veered off course like that during a presentation. And *why,*—despite the fact that her mind knew Matt
Davidson was insufferable—was her body not falling in
line with the program? His insinuation that she was trying to charm Jack Witherspoon with more than her creative ideas was insulting and infuriating. But what made it
even more infuriating was the fact that while ninety-nine
percent of her was outraged at his innuendo, there was
unfortunately that one percent—some errant feminine
chromosome she was beginning to dislike intensely—
that quickened at the notion that Matt thought anything
about her was sexy.

"Augh!" She plunged her fingers into her hair—her
loose, *sexy* hair—and fisted her hands. She squeezed her
eyes tight, hoping to ward off the sound of her excruci-
atingly honest inner voice, but it tapped her on the shoulder.

Hey, Jilly, her inner voice said. *Let's be honest here, okay?*

You did *wear a skirt and heels and your hair down and red lips with the thought of enticing a man—but that man wasn't Jack Witherspoon.*

She blew out a long sigh filled with resignation and frustration. As much as she'd like to lie to herself, what was the point? While she wouldn't compromise herself by dressing sexy for a client, deep down she knew she'd tried to look more alluring than she normally would, hoping that Matt would notice. And obviously he had. And obviously he thought she was playing the sexy card to win Jack's favor.

And yes, while that was insulting, she couldn't really blame him. After all, he didn't know her. He had no way of knowing that she would never stoop to something like that. That her sense of fair play and her integrity balked at such underhanded tactics. That she'd rather lose fairly than win unfairly. All he really knew about her through their frequent head-butting was that she was highly competitive, extremely ambitious, and wanted very much to land the ARC account. That, coupled with the fact that many women—and men—in their industry did use sex to get ahead…well, it really wasn't unreasonable or unthinkable that such an assumption would cross his mind. If their situations were reversed, she would have thought the same thing.

She rose and paced to the window. The thick green drapes were pushed back, allowing daylight to flood the room. Drawing aside the sheer, cream curtain panel, she looked out at the snow-covered vineyards. Row upon row of bare vines, held in place by thick wooden stakes and a trio of horizontal cables, stood at attention like a battalion of soldiers. With the harvest season over, the vines resembled thick stems with gnarled fingers pointing upward toward the gray, snow-leaden sky.

Fat white snowflakes drifted downward, beckoning Jilly to come out and play in the winter wonderland. Since she wasn't meeting Jack until three, and she had no desire to remain in this room where the tantalizing fragrance of Matt's musky cologne still lingered, she gave in to the beckoning. She crossed to the closet and pulled out her favorite pair of jeans and a thick, cable-knit sweater, ignoring how disturbingly intimate Matt's clothes looked hung next to hers.

She changed in quick order, slipped her suit onto a hanger, and was just preparing to lace up her sturdy snow boots when she heard the door lock click. She looked up just as Matt, laptop case in hand, strode into the room.

He halted at the sight of her, and for several seconds silence swelled as they stared at each other. Annoyance at his earlier assumption mingled with a tingling awareness of his dark good looks and masculinity. Whew. He might be a pain in the butt, but there was no getting away from the fact that he was a damn fine-looking pain in the butt.

Finally she glanced pointedly at her watch. "It's barely nine-fifteen. Your breakfast meeting didn't take very long."

"Jack sent a message that he was delayed and rescheduled our appointment for ten. Thought I'd come back up here where it's quiet and review my presentation."

She raised her brows. "Are you sure you didn't come back up here to check on my whereabouts? To see if maybe *I* was what had delayed Jack?"

He hesitated a moment, then said, "I have to admit, I'm relieved to discover you here."

A humorless laugh escaped her. "Don't you mean surprised?"

"No. I mean relieved." He shrugged. "With maybe a little surprise thrown in."

Humph. For an answer, she returned her attention to lacing up her boots. "I'll be out of here in just a minute."

"Fine." Without another word, he crossed to the desk, set his laptop on the polished oak surface, then flicked the On button. Peeking at him from under her lashes, she watched him settle himself in the chintz-covered wing chair, then pull a disk from his laptop case and insert it into the computer. Seconds later a frown pulled down his brows. His gaze scanned the screen, and his frown turned into a scowl.

She heard his fingers tapping away on the keyboard, then a muffled curse. She pressed her lips together and kept lacing. Clearly something was wrong. Well, too bad. It wasn't her problem. Whatever disaster had befallen Matt Davidson, he most likely deserved it.

Done with her lacing, she looked up, and her gaze involuntarily flicked over to him. His face was pale, his lips flattened into a thin line, and a muscle ticked in his jaw.

Before she could clamp a hand over her mouth, she found herself asking, "Problem?"

With his gaze still glued to the screen, he dragged his hands down his face. "Ever have the day from hell?"

"Frequently. Today, for instance, is a front-runner, thanks to you."

He shot her a glare. "Ha ha. You're a real laugh a minute."

"Thank ya, thank ya verra much," she said in her best Elvis impersonation. "I'll be here all weekend. So what's wrong?"

"Well, yesterday was my latest day from hell. Everything that *could* go wrong, did." His gaze returned to the screen, and his fingers resumed typing. "And I've just discovered that the day from hell simply keeps on giving and giving."

"Meaning what?"

"My laptop crashed yesterday. Got infected with the Missionary Position virus that's wreaking havoc everywhere."

Sympathy instantly overrode Jilly's annoyance and she winced. "Ouch. I've heard that virus is especially bad."

"You're not kidding. I turned on the computer and this little dancing naked guy appeared, then *pffft*," he snapped his fingers, "little dancing naked guy gave an evil chuckle, said, 'You're screwed,' then proceeded to hump his way across the screen and delete all my files."

Her eyes widened. "Yikes. That *is* bad—and undignified to boot."

He shot her a glare. "Don't you dare laugh."

"I wouldn't dream of it. My computer got fried by the Lollipop virus last year, so I know how awful it is. Did you bring the laptop to Maxximum's IT department? I took my machine to them when it was infected, and they were able to recover most of my files."

"I left it with them yesterday afternoon and filled out an emergency requisition for a new laptop." He nodded toward the machine in front of him. "This is it."

"And I gather that there's something wrong with it?"

"You could say that. It appears that whoever loaded the software onto this particular set neglected to load any of the standard word processing programs."

"You're kidding." She crossed to the desk, then looked at the screen over his shoulder.

"I wish I was. Look." He pointed to the icons. "Not there."

"Did you search through the program files?"

"Twice. Not there." He tunneled his fingers through

his hair and groaned. "I should have suspected something would go wrong since the guy in IT yesterday was a temp. Obviously the temp from hell. A perfect match for the day from hell." A very unamused sounding laugh erupted from him. "Well, that's going to delay my presentation for Jack—at least until I can get to a computer store and buy the software I need and install it. God knows where the nearest computer store is. This area isn't exactly a booming metropolis." He glanced over his shoulder at the heavy snowfall visible through the window. "And with all this snow, the roads are most likely a mess."

"The last forecast I heard predicted from one to a hundred and twenty-five inches of snow," she said with a half smile.

"Well, at least the weatherman has a chance of being right by covering his bases that way."

"Can't you give Jack a hard copy of your presentation?"

"Except for a few sketches, I don't have one." He popped the disk from his useless laptop and held it up. "It's all on here. On a fabulous—if I may say so myself—PowerPoint slide show." He shifted in his chair and looked at her over his shoulder. "Seems I'm temporarily out of commission. Nice break for you."

She studied him for several seconds. She could almost feel the frustration emanating off him. She should be happy. Should be celebrating having this small advantage handed to her on a silver platter. But her conscience kicked her in the butt, forcing her feet to carry her across the room. She picked up her laptop and returned to him, setting her computer on the desk.

"You can use mine."

He stared at her, his expression a combination of suspicion, amazement, and confusion as his gaze alternated between her and her laptop. Finally he asked, "What's the catch?"

"No catch."

His eyes narrowed. "There's always a catch."

Annoyance prickled her. "Sheesh. You sure are suspicious. Look, if you don't want to use it, fine. You can sit here until the spring thaw, or hitch your car up to a team of mush dogs and try to get to a computer store. Makes no difference to me."

"Why would you let me use it?"

She planted her palms on the desk and leaned forward until less than a foot separated their faces. His gaze dropped briefly to her lips, and she noted the unmistakable desire darkening his eyes. She ignored the quickening of her pulse in response.

"Why? You know what, Matt? I'm not sure, especially since I don't particularly like you. Maybe it's because if the situation were reversed, I'm not certain you'd show me the same courtesy and I want you to feel guilty about that. Maybe it's because I've been in a similar situation and someone was kind enough to help me out and I just want to pay it forward. Maybe it's because I want to prove to you that I mean it when I say I play fair. Or maybe it's because when I win the ARC account, I don't want to hear any whining from you that I only got it because you couldn't play your 'A' game due to technical difficulties."

She remained leaning on the desk, heart beating hard against her ribs as they studied each other, tension and awareness bouncing between them. He clearly felt that tension and awareness, too. She could see it in his eyes.

Finally he said, "Aren't you afraid I'll look through your files?"

"They're password protected."

"Now who's being suspicious?"

"I prefer to call it cautious. Besides, you have the corner marketed on suspicion. Are you suspicious of everyone, or am I the only proud recipient of your doubtfulness?"

"Don't take it personally. It's not just you. And I have my reasons."

Something flickered in his eyes, the shadows of past hurts, piquing her curiosity, but she didn't ask. "Well, that's good to know. I think." Straightening, she headed toward the closet where she pulled out her black goosedown winter coat. When she turned around, she found him standing directly in front of her. Clutching her coat to her chest as if to ward off the sensual vibes he threw off, she backed up a step. Her shoulders hit the wall.

"Where are you going?" he asked in a husky voice that brought to mind candlelight and satin sheets.

"Outside."

"It's cold and snowing."

"I like the cold and snow." Yup, something icy would be really welcome right about now.

He reached out and plucked her coat from her fingers, then held it out by the shoulders for her, a gentlemanly gesture she'd thought died with the dinosaur. Turning her back toward him, she slowly slipped her arms into the sleeves, trying without success to ignore his disturbing nearness. After he settled the coat on her shoulders, she turned to face him once again. She was about to thank him, but the intense look in his eyes obliterated every thought from her head. She remained silent, stuck in place like an insect trapped in a web.

A good ten seconds of silence passed. Then he reached out and trailed a single fingertip down her cheek. Her breath caught at the feathery touch, and a trail of heat ignited on her skin where he'd touched her.

"You've surprised me, Jilly," he said softly, his gaze searching her face. "And I don't particularly like surprises."

She blinked and swallowed. "Gee, thanks."

He shook his head and frowned. "I'm sorry. I didn't mean that the way it sounded. What I meant is that the unexpected unsettles me. And you...well, you're not what I...expected." His hand lowered to his side, then he stepped back, and she released a breath she hadn't even realized she held.

"Thank you, Jilly," he said, still studying her face, as if trying to solve a great puzzle. "I really appreciate you loaning me your laptop. Believe me, I am well aware that not everyone would be so generous."

"You're welcome. See you later." With a quick smile, she left the room, walking swiftly toward the elevator, anxious to put as much space between her and Matt as possible. And even more anxious to get outside where it was cold, because she was feeling an uncomfortable warmth—warmth that had nothing to do with the resort's heating system and everything to do with her roommate. Yes, the farther away she stayed from Matt, the better off she'd be. But what on earth was she going to do tonight when they would once again have to share a bed?

MATT WATCHED THE DOOR CLOSE behind Jilly. When it clicked shut, he tipped back his head, closed his eyes, and groaned.

This was *so* not good. Damn it, from the moment he'd walked into this room last night, his world had gotten turned upside down. And every time he managed to set it back on his axis, she did something else to throw him all off-kilter again. Like wear black satin lingerie to bed. And leave her long hair down. And accentuate her gorgeous lips with kiss-me red. And loan him her laptop.

Would he have done the same for her if the situations had been reversed? As much as he'd like to tell to himself that he'd have chosen the high road, in his heart he knew he wouldn't have. While he wouldn't do anything to directly sabotage Jilly, he definitely would have taken advantage of her misfortune—a realization that left a bad taste in his mouth. Especially when it hit him that only a year ago, before he'd been stabbed in the back by Tricia and his former best friend, he most likely would have acted as Jilly had. Probably. At least he liked to think so.

But Jilly had made that generous gesture with little or no hesitation—despite the fact that she ''didn't particularly like him.''

Humph. "Well, I don't particularly like you, either," he muttered. He certainly didn't like that she had him tied up in all these damn knots. And he definitely didn't like that her generous gesture was making him examine his own behavior and realize it was coming up short. And he *really* didn't like the disturbing suspicion that maybe he didn't dislike her at all.

He blew out a long, frustrated breath. Just as she'd suspected, he *had* come back to the room to see if she was here, to see if she was the reason Jack had rescheduled their meeting. And when he'd found her in the room, he was far more relieved than he cared to admit. The thought of her seducing Jack Witherspoon bothered him a hell of a lot more than it should have—on a gutwrenching, personal level it shouldn't have.

He was feeling things for Jilly that he wanted no part of. Heat. Desire. Admiration. Things he'd vowed never to allow himself to feel again for a co-worker. He knew where that led. Never again. He needed to remember his vow: No more fishing off the company pier. He needed to concentrate on Jack Witherspoon and ARC. And he needed to forget all about Jilly Taylor.

Then his gaze fell to the bed...the bed they'd be sharing in only a matter of hours. Damn. That was going to make it very difficult indeed to forget about Jilly Taylor.

SHORTLY AFTER ONE O'CLOCK that afternoon, Jilly walked up the long, curved driveway leading to Chateau Fontaine. She'd spent a few head-clearing hours walking a half mile up the road to the quaint town, strolling through the cozy shops, then enjoying lunch and a cappuccino at a café. The snow had stopped, and the cold, still air had done wonders to clear the Matt Davidson-induced cobwebs from her brain and shift her priorities back into some semblance of order.

Cool, aloof, and professional would be her watch words for the remainder of the weekend. Clearly her hormones were suffering from some sort of glandular imbalance brought on by nine months, three weeks and nineteen days of neglect, which explained this ridiculous, unwanted physical attraction to Matt. Well, next week that would change. She'd call an emergency summit meeting with Kate and together they'd set about finding her an acceptable man—or two—to date. Once her social life started humming again, she'd forget all about Matt.

As if the thought of him had conjured him up, she saw Matt making his way from the parking lot toward the hotel. Slowing her pace, she looked him over. One hand was jammed into the pocket of a black ski jacket. In the other hand he held a white plastic bag that proclaimed he'd visited The Computer Warehouse. Faded jeans hugged his long legs, and snow crunched beneath his sturdy brown Timberland boots. He looked big and strong and sexy and—she shook her head to adjust her runaway thoughts. And completely...undelicious. Yup, that's what he was—the exact *opposite* of delicious.

He must have felt the weight of her regard, because he turned and their eyes met. His steps slowed, but then he shifted his direction and walked toward her.

Her stupid heart rate kicked up a few beats per minute, and her hormones perked up their ears. She shot her hormones an inward frown and told them to take a hike.

"Don't tell me you're still out here from this morning," Matt said as he neared her. "I've only been outside for a few minutes and already I feel like a Popsicle." He pulled his hand from his pocket, cupped his fingers near his mouth and blew to warm them.

Jilly's wayward gaze wandered over his dark, wind-blown hair, and she clenched her fingers inside her gloves to squelch the urge to brush back a wayward lock that fell over his forehead. Ruddy color from the cold stained his cheeks, lending him a very outdoorsy, masculine appearance. He looked incredibly appealing, and all the resolutions she'd just spent the past three hours making evaporated like a puff of steam.

Darn it, why did this particular man have to be so damn attractive? He shifted his feet, drawing her gaze down his long legs. Yikes. Last time she'd seen a guy fill out a pair of jeans that nicely had been...never. Her thought processes derailed, and her mind executed a mental striptease, peeling off his heavy coat and sweater. Whew, he sure looked good. She imagined sliding those Levi's down his long legs, then slipping off his boxer briefs—with her teeth.

A feverish flush washed over her, no doubt generating

enough heat to melt the snow beneath her feet. She was going to look pretty stupid standing out here in a big puddle of water.

"Penny for your thoughts."

Her gaze jerked up to his, and she stilled at the speculative interest simmering in his eyes. Damn. Bad enough to indulge in such unacceptable fantasies, but it was bury-your-head-in-the-snow embarrassing for him to catch her indulging.

She attempted a laugh, inwardly cringing at the shaky sound she produced. "I, uh was just imagining how good you'd look…" *naked* "…covered in snow." *Yeah, that's the ticket.*

He cocked a brow, his gaze filling with a wicked gleam and alternating between her and the pile of snow near his feet. "Funny, I was thinking how great *you'd* look all covered with snow."

"Oh, yeah? Wanna put that theory to the test?"

He stroked his chin. "Hmmm. An intriguing invitation, and one I think I'll take you up on. And seeing how nice you were about loaning me your laptop, I'll even let you win."

"You won't have to let me win. I'm gonna whip your butt."

"Okay. But after that we're gonna have a snowball fight." A slow smile curved his lips and her heart tripped. Pointing to the deserted area beyond the parking lot, he said, "Shall we take this to yon empty field?"

"Lead on, sucker—uh, I mean, oh wise one."

He chuckled and they walked toward the parking lot. Glancing down at his bag, she said, "I see you found a computer store."

"Yup. Bought the software I needed. I was on my way up to the room to install it." He looked down at her, his eyes serious. "Thanks again for the laptop loan. That was really decent of you."

"I'm sure you don't mean to sound so surprised that I'd do something decent. How'd the presentation go?"

"Very well. He liked my ideas."

"He liked mine, too."

"I know. I liked yours as well." He shot her a cocky smile. "But I like mine better."

"Well, I wouldn't know, seeing as how I didn't see yours."

"Would you like to see mine, Jilly?"

Something in the husky timbre of his voice made her suddenly wonder if they were still talking about his presentation. "Sure," she said breezily, "if you'd like to show me."

Something flared in his eyes, something that indicated very clearly that he'd like to show her more than his presentation. And God help her, she wanted to take a good, long look at whatever he wanted to show her.

He huffed out a long breath that formed a cloudy vapor. After several long seconds of silence, he cleared his throat, then asked, "So...what's the prize for winning this snowball fight?"

How about a long, slow, deep kiss? Beating back the heat-inducing thought, she held up her small, shiny red shopping bag. "I'm willing to put up the box of candy I bought in town, which, I'll have you know, because they're my favorites, I wouldn't dream of risking if I wasn't completely confident of my winning."

"What kind of candy?"

"Homemade chocolate-covered marshmallows."

He shot her an odd look. "They're *my* favorite."

"Oh, sure."

At her dubious expression, he added, "Really. Always

have been. Not that I admit that to a lot of people since marshmallows aren't exactly he-man like, but there you have it. Actually, growing up, it worked out well. I didn't eat my sister's Oreos and she didn't mess with my Mallomars." A wolfish grin curved his lips. "It's going to be *sweet* indeed to relieve you of your chocolates."

"Dream on, Marshmallow-boy. And just what do you plan to wager?"

"What do you want?"

"What have you got?"

"Since I'm so confident of my victory..." He leaned toward her, and his masculine scent, mixed with winter cold, invaded her head, fogging her brain cells. "If you beat me, I'll give you anything you want, Jilly."

5

IF YOU BEAT ME, I'll give you anything you want, Jilly.

Matt's provocative words reverberated through her mind, whipping up a tornado of sensual images, proving beyond any doubt what she wanted. Forcing those images aside, she murmured, "Anything I want? Excellent. I hope you've got ten grand lying around that you won't miss."

"Ah, but I'm banking on you using that sense of fair play you pride yourself on." The expression in his dark blue eyes curled her toes inside her boots. "I'll give you whatever you want, Jilly. Within reason."

Oh, boy. She knew what she wanted—or at least her screaming hormones did. They wanted a bout of sweaty, mindless sex with Matt. Good grief, it was only about seventeen degrees outside, but she felt like she was melting from the inside out—and he hadn't even touched her. What the heck would happen if he put his hands on her? *Don't even think about it.*

As they neared the end of the parking lot, he paused beside a shiny, black Lexus that had been cleaned of snow, pulled a key ring from his pocket, then clicked open the automatic door locks.

Opening the driver's door, he set his bag on the beige leather seat. "In the spirit of fair play, would you like to leave your bag of candy in my car?"

"Sure." She smiled. "If you'll let me hold the keys."

"Now who's being suspicious?"

"I'm not going to risk you holding my marshmallows hostage."

"I won't have to. I'm going to win them fair and square."

"Then you have nothing to worry about."

"How do I know you won't hold my car hostage? A box of candy versus my Lexus." He shook his head. "Doesn't seem quite fair."

"You haven't tasted these chocolates." Reaching into the bag, she pulled out a red and green striped box and flipped the lid. Sliding off her purple wool glove, she picked up a chocolate square and held it out to him. "Taste."

Instead of taking his hands out of his pocket, he leaned down and took a bite of the morsel. His lips brushed over her fingertips, freezing her in place at the same time fire shot up her arm.

Straightening to his full height, he chewed slowly, his gaze steady on hers, while she stared with an expression that probably resembled a starstruck adolescent who'd just found herself standing next to Ben Affleck. Good grief, Matt Davidson possessed the sexiest mouth she'd ever seen. And seeing it wrapped around her chocolate was almost more than she could stand. Before she could recover, however, he reached out, lightly clasped her wrist between his strong fingers, then brought her hand to his mouth. Staring into her eyes, he gently drew the other half of the chocolate into his mouth. His tongue brushed over her fingertips and desire hit her so hard she felt woozy.

She watched him chew, half her attention fixed on his beautiful mouth, the other half on the pulse-quickening feel of his skin touching hers where he still held her wrist.

After he swallowed, he said softly, "Delicious."

Unable to find her voice, she merely nodded.

"That sample makes me want more."

Yeah, me, too. She drew in a much-needed breath, slipped her hand from his, and gave herself a mental shake. Flipping the box closed, she resettled the candy in her shopping bag, then placed the bag on the front seat. "I will refrain from saying I told you so. Unfortunately for you, that's all you get."

He smiled. "Until I win."

She smiled back and held out her hand. "Keys?"

He closed the car door, clicked the remote to lock the doors, then dropped the keys in her palm. She tucked the key ring in her pocket, then resolutely slipped her glove back on. After offering him a jaunty salute, she jogged the short distance to the end of the parking lot.

Matt took a few seconds to pull in a breath and get his raging libido under control. His palm still tingled from the warmth of her skin. His head still swam from the clean laundry scent that wafted from her skin, tempting him to lean closer and breathe her in. His groin still felt tight where his damn jeans were strangling him, and his—

Splat!

He looked down. And his chest was covered in snow.

Another snowball smacked him on the shoulder, knocking him from his stupor. Looking up, he saw her, half-hidden behind a tree about twenty feet away. "Hey!" he protested, starting forward. "We haven't gone over the rules."

"The one with the most snow on him loses," she called. Another missile caught him in the thigh, and he made a mad dash for a slender tree that stood about fifteen feet away from hers. She hit him in the ass with another snowball before he ducked for cover.

"No fair," he yelled, furiously packing a snowball, and cursing that he wasn't wearing gloves. "I didn't know we were starting."

"European rules. They're rough. Get used to it." A snowball hit his tree trunk just above his head, spraying snow on his face as the missile broke apart. Jeez, the woman had skill. She had aim like a major league pitcher. The Mets could use her.

He built up his arsenal to twelve hastily made snowballs, managing to avoid most of the barrage that she launched at him.

"What do you have, sixteen arms?" he asked. "How are you making those snowballs so fast?"

"Ha! Like I'm going to tell you. But the fact that I'm wearing gloves helps."

Another ball of white whizzed by his ear. "How about giving me one of those gloves?"

"Forget it. Not when there's chocolate on the line."

"What happened to fair play and all that?"

"All's fair in snowball war."

Peeking around the tree trunk, he took aim and threw, catching her on the arm. "Take that."

A snowball exploded just below his chin. He glared at her, and she favored him with an evil chuckle.

"You're going down, Davidson."

"Not without a fight."

Over the next ten minutes, he managed to get in a few good shots, but with his fingers growing numb, and her freakin' dead-eye aim, he had to face the fact that he only had one chance of winning. Gathering up his last few snowballs, he crouched low and ran like hell toward her.

"I'm storming the citadel," he yelled, furiously throwing his remaining weapons.

"You're toast," she yelled back, pelting him at close range with a double whammy that caught him in the shoulder and the chin.

With a low growl, he caught her around the waist as she bent to grab another handful of snow. She squealed, and tried to break away, throwing him off balance. Unable to catch himself, he fell forward, landing half on top of her just as she fell, face down, in the snow.

He immediately pushed himself up onto his hands. "Jeez, Jilly, are you okay?"

She rolled over and glared at him through snowflake flecked lashes. "Yeah, I'm swell."

"Did I hurt you?"

She wiped her wet face with the back of her glove, but as her gloves were wet, it didn't help much. "Only my pride."

He exhaled his relief. "I'm sorry. I didn't mean to tackle you—you threw me off balance." His gaze wandered over her and he grinned. "Looks like I win."

Her eyes goggled. "*You?* You, who couldn't hit the side of an elephant with a handful of rice? You, who couldn't hit water if you fell out of a boat?"

"Ah, but you said that the one with the most snow on him loses, and you—" his gaze traveled pointedly down her snow-covered front "—clearly have more snow on you."

"Only because you flung me face down in the snow."

"I didn't fling. I tripped. And only because you squealed and flailed your arms around like a girl."

"That wasn't a squeal, it was a shout of surprise at being manhandled by the enemy. And I wasn't flailing, I was trying to regain my balance after you knocked me off

my feet, you big klutz. And here's a news flash for you—
I *am* a girl.''

He looked down into those big, golden-brown eyes,
and it suddenly struck him more forcefully than ever that
she was very much a girl. And that he was very much a
guy. And that all his guy stuff was pressed against the
length of all her girl stuff.

Desire sucker-punched him in the gut. She must have
read it in his eyes because she suddenly went completely
still beneath him, and awareness and heat flared in her
gaze.

He meant to shift off her, surely he did, but his muscles
refused to move. Still, certainly he would have pushed
himself off her—but then her gaze dropped to his mouth.

That look touched him like a caress, and he bit back a
groan of want. Before all the reasons he shouldn't raised
their voices, he leaned down and touched his mouth to
hers. Certainly he meant it only to be a light kiss, experi-
mental, but after a few seconds her lips—those beautiful,
soft, tempting lips—parted, and her tongue brushed
against his. And all bets were off.

He moaned—or was that her?—and slanted his mouth
over hers, his tongue tasting all the warm, secret lusciousness of her. Every part of him that had been icy cold
only seconds earlier, heated like he'd stepped into a
brushfire. Clearly she'd sampled her candy earlier because she tasted like chocolate—sweet and delicious.
And everything about her, from the feel of her pressed
against him to her luscious taste, made him want to de-
vour her.

The frosty, wet wool of her gloved fingers brushed his
nape, shooting a shiver down his spine, and rousing his
drugged senses enough to remind him of where he was.
And whom he was with.

Slowly lifting his head, he looked down into eyes darkened with arousal, yet flickering with the same wary expression he knew was reflected in his own eyes.

He needed to say something—preferably something along the lines of *boy, that was a big mistake we'd better not let happen again*—but damned if he could find his voice. All he could do was stare at her and fight the overwhelming urge to kiss her again. And again.

Finally she cleared her throat. "I have a confession to make."

"What's that?" he said in a croaky, husky voice he didn't recognize.

"I'd...wondered."

He didn't pretend to misunderstand. "Well, in that case, I have a confession to make as well. I'd wondered, too."

"Finding out probably wasn't a great idea."

"Right."

"We can sum that kiss up in four words: severe lack of judgment."

"Right."

"And now that we've satisfied our mutual curiosity, we can just...?" Her voice trailed off, and her gaze searched his, as if seeking the correct ending to her sentence.

"We can just forget about it." His lips said the words, but he had a sinking feeling that if he lived to be a hundred, he'd never forget that kiss.

"Forget about it. Exactly. That would definitely be best."

"Definitely."

Forcing himself to move, he rolled off her, then rose to his feet. Extending his hands, he helped her to stand.

"Your hands are like ice, Matt."

He looked down at his reddened fingers with a rueful expression. "Yeah. I think rigor mortis has set in—that's Latin for 'I should have worn gloves.'" He thrust his hands into his jacket pockets, telling himself it was to warm them, but it was really to keep from drawing her into his arms and seeing what kiss number two would be like.

Glancing down, he saw a perfectly made snowball resting at the base of the tree. "You forgot one," he said, indicating the missile with a jerk of his head.

She noted the snowball, then smiled at him. "That was the one that was going to finish you off."

"Much as I hate to admit it, you'd already finished me off. If there were an Olympic snowball fight team, you'd bring home the gold. Where'd you learn to throw snowballs like that?"

"I played centerfield for my high school softball team. We won four state championships." She batted her eyelashes. "Did I neglect to mention that?"

"Uh-uh. And if I weren't so impressed by your ability, I'd be royally pissed. Personally, I think you should give up advertising and try out for the major leagues."

"Hmmm. That would be one way to eliminate me from the competition."

He laid one frozen hand over his heart. "I say that strictly as a baseball fan whose beloved sport is badly in need of your skills."

"I'm sure you like to tell yourself that."

"Well, one thing I don't like to tell myself is that you whipped my butt, but you did." He bowed from the waist. "I am vanquished." His gaze drifted over her lips and he pushed aside the disturbing thought that she'd conquered him in more ways than one.

She looked smug, but at least she didn't say I told you

so. "Looks like you're going to have to give me whatever I want."

"Within reason," he reminded her. "I guess that wasn't such a smart wager on my account. Of course, I didn't know I was dealing with a ringer."

"If you'd asked, I would have told you. I'm good at a lot of things."

I bet you are. And just thinking about some of the things he'd bet she was good at rushed blood to his groin.

She pulled his key ring from her pocket and, twirling the shiny silver circle around her finger, led the way back to his Lexus.

After retrieving her shopping bag from the front seat, she tossed him the keys. "I'm heading up to the room to change into dry clothes. I'm meeting Jack at three for a tour of the winery."

Something snaked through him that felt suspiciously like jealousy—and it had nothing to do with the fact that she was making inroads with the potential client. "I see. I'll be sure to stay out of your way."

"Thank you."

"I'm meeting Jack at five in the bar."

"All right. I'll be sure to stay out of *your* way—assuming you've done the same for me."

"You really are very suspicious, Jilly, especially given how I conceded that you won the snowball fight even though you had more snow on you."

She cocked a brow. "Do you want a rematch?"

"Hell, no. One slice of humble pie is quite enough, thank you."

A wicked gleam flickered in her eyes. "Speaking of things to eat, I think I'll have one of my delicious chocolate-covered marshmallows while I'm changing my clothes."

Damn, but she was cute. And alluring. And tempting. And sexy as hell. And he didn't want her to be. Arranging his features into a frown, he said, "Hey, I have a car. I could just drive to that candy store and buy my own box of chocolate-covered marshmallows. A *bigger* box."

"Ah, but they wouldn't taste as good as the ones in *this* box. Because these are the spoils of war. The sweets of victory. The ambrosia of triumph. The—"

"Yeah, yeah, yeah, I get the picture." He set his hands on her shoulders and gave her a gentle urging toward the resort. "Go on, scram with your chocolates, before I use my superior masculine strength and just grab them from you."

"I'd like to see you try." She smiled. "I'm a black belt."

"Figures."

"You're not coming back to the room?"

"I'll be along in a few minutes. I need to make a call on my cell. That'll give you enough time to change in privacy."

Their gazes met, and he swore something electric passed between them. Something intimate and knowing. Something that indicated they both knew that him being in the room while she changed her clothes was a temptation they shouldn't risk.

"See you," she said. With a breezy wave, she walked across the parking lot, then disappeared from his view through the revolving door.

When she was gone from his sight, he drew what seemed like his first easy breath in an hour. Thank God she was gone.

Too bad she wasn't forgotten.

SHORTLY AFTER FIVE O'CLOCK that evening, Jilly stood near the window in her room, looking out over the snow-covered landscape. Jabbing Kate's phone number into her cell phone pad, Jilly tapped her foot and prayed Kate was home.

"I need help," Jilly said into the phone the instant Kate answered. "This weekend is turning into a complete disaster."

"Uh-oh. I'm listening. Spill it."

She told her the entire debacle—of her boss's trickery, and of being forced to share room 312 with Matt. She concluded by saying, "I just spent the last two hours touring the winery and going to a tasting with Jack Witherspoon, but this situation with Matt has me so frazzled, I couldn't tell you if I'd tasted a merlot or a chardonnay."

"Didn't I tell you?" Kate asked. "When you least anticipate it, something unexpected will happen and—*poof!*—your world will be turned upside down."

"Great. That doesn't help."

"Sorry. What does Matt look like with his shirt off?"

Jilly closed her eyes. "Incredible."

"Have you done more than look at him?"

"He kissed me."

"And?"

"I kissed him back."

"And?"

Jilly blew out a long breath. "It was the sort of kiss you'd like to have last for three weeks instead of three minutes. We're talking melting the polar ice caps."

"Oh, my. What was his reaction?"

"Let's just say he wasn't anatomically aloof." A frustrated moan rumbled in Jilly's throat. "The problem is, he's got my hormones all out of whack and I want to do a hell of a lot more than just kiss him."

"And that's a problem because...?"

"You even need to ask? Because we work together. Because he's the only thing standing between me and the ARC account. Because once I win this account, I'll be his *boss*. How awkward would *that* be if we'd slept together? And even if I could ignore all that, he's just not my type. He's one of those guys who always has to be in charge. You know how I feel about that."

"I do," Kate said softly. "But, Jilly, you're not your mom. I think you're losing sight of the fact that we're talking about *sleeping* with Matt, not walking down the aisle with him."

"True. But having an affair with him—God, that would make working together impossible—especially after it ended."

"Yes, but let's face it, with the sexual spark that's clearly crackling between you, it's going to be awkward anyway."

"But more awkward if I know what he looks like, and feels like, naked." A shiver ran through her at the wealth of images that sentence conjured up.

"Not necessarily. Maybe if you indulge in an affair with him this weekend, your curiosity will be satisfied, and then you'll be able to forget him. No more wondering, it'll be over and done with. As long as you both go into it understanding the ground rules."

"You mean like we'll satisfy our lust this weekend only, then never speak of this 'at the winery' incident again?"

"Exactly. Listen, Jilly. You *really* need a man to take care of you in the sack. Now. Before you dry up and blow away. And as far as I know, no one's kindled the least bit of interest in you in a long time. If Matt lights your fire, then maybe you should give him the matches—at least for this weekend."

"Okay, you're not really helping here. I called you to talk me *out* of this craziness."

"Oh. Sorry. How's this? You don't want to do something that could in any way mess with your career or make an already awkward situation worse. Matt is definitely Mr. Hands Off."

"Exactly." There. She knew talking with Kate would get her head back on straight.

"But there's no denying that you need a man."

"Much as I hate to agree with you, you're right. I won't be back at work until Tuesday. But as soon as I hit Manhattan, I'm looking for a man to put out this damn fire that Matt started."

"Atta girl. Between the two of us, we'll find you someone. I'll enlist Ben's help as well."

"Too bad Ben doesn't have a brother."

"He does. But he's a priest."

"Right. Too bad Ben doesn't have a brother who isn't a priest." Jilly sighed. "Still, even if we find me a man, there's this slight confidence problem."

"Meaning?"

Jilly dragged her free hand through her hair. "I'm... nervous. I haven't had sex in so long, you could nickname me Rusty."

Kate laughed. "Don't worry. It's as natural as breathing."

"Sure, says a woman who has fabulous sex on a regular basis."

"And soon you will be, too."

"I can only hope you're—" She turned around and her words cut off as if they'd been sliced with a machete.

Matt, looking tall, dark and delicious in a pair of charcoal-gray dress pants and a cream, crewneck sweater, leaned against the closed door, an unreadable expression on his face.

Mortification consumed her in one gulp, rushing a flush of heat up her back. "I...I've got to go," she said into the phone, her voice coming out in a croak.

"Uh-oh. Did he come in?"

"Yeah." The question was, *when* had he entered the room? Ack! How much had he overheard?

"Okay. Chin up. Take deep cleansing breaths, and if all else fails, take a cold shower. Call me tomorrow, all right?"

"You bet." Her gaze steady on Matt's, she slowly hung up the receiver. "I didn't hear you come in."

"Sorry. I didn't mean to startle you."

"How long were you standing there?"

"Not long."

Her eyes narrowed. "What did you hear?"

"Nothing."

His blank expression gave nothing away. She prayed he was telling the truth. Otherwise she'd have to move to another state. Possibly another country. "Aren't you supposed to be with Jack now in the bar?"

"We'd just ordered drinks when I realized I forgot my cell phone. I'm expecting an important call." Pushing off from the door, he walked to the night table and picked up his small phone.

Her brows shot upward. Personally she would have let her voice mail pick up the call rather than interrupt time with a client as valuable as Jack, and it surprised her—and pricked her curiosity—that Matt wouldn't do the same. Who was he expecting such an important call from?

"Jack suggested that the three of us have dinner together this evening," Matt said.

"Oh? When did he say that?"

"About five minutes ago, in the bar. He told me to extend the invite to you if you were in the room."

Another embarrassed flush snaked up her back. "So he knows we're sharing a room?"

"Well, it doesn't take a genius to figure out that if we're both in room 312—and the chances of there being more than one room 312 are pretty slim—we're roommates. I explained about the reservation mix-up. He thought it was pretty funny."

"Yeah. It's hysterical." She shot him a narrow-eyed look. "What if I hadn't been in the room?"

"Jack would have called and left a message."

"Where and when is dinner?"

"Six-thirty, in the resort's restaurant."

"I'll be there," she said, refusing to acknowledge the sudden leap her heart performed—a leap that had nothing to do with the prospect of dining with Jack Witherspoon. "At least we won't have to dodge each other all evening."

"Right. Listen, as long as you're here, I want to pay my debt of honor." He crossed to the desk and opened his laptop. "I owe you a look at my presentation."

Her surprise must have shown because he smiled. "Obviously you thought I'd conveniently forget but, if nothing else, I'm a man of my word. Take a look."

Jilly joined him and peered over his shoulder, watching the clever five-minute PowerPoint slide show which highlighted Matt's slogan. "ARC Software," he said softly as the words appeared on the screen. "Load it, Launch it, Love it."

Heat suffused her. Whew. The way he murmured his slogan in that husky, suggestive voice made *Load it,*

Launch it, Love it sound like something she'd want to experience with him in the dark. While they were naked.

And there was nothing wrong with that. Everyone knew sex sold. Damn. She wished she'd hated his presentation, wished it were awful. Wished she could lie and tell him that. Instead she said, "Very nice. I'm impressed."

"Thank you. I'm glad we're even now."

"Not exactly even. You still owe me for the snowball fight."

"I was hoping you'd forget."

"Not a chance. In fact, maybe I'll ask for another snowball fight."

"I hope not. I'm apparently not very good at them."

She smiled. "I know. That's why I like to play with you."

He laughed. "Well, I anxiously await to hear what you desire so I can pay my debt." Shooting her a snappy salute, he headed toward the door. "I'll see you at six-thirty." With that, he left the room, leaving Jilly to stare at the door through which he'd just departed.

What I desire? Good grief. She pushed her mental rewind button and cringed at what she'd said to Kate. The thought of Matt knowing that he had her all hot and bothered and that she'd been thinking about having sex with him—yikes.

Thank God he hadn't overheard any of *that*.

6

SITTING AT A COZY TABLE tucked in a quiet corner of Le Cabernet Bistro, Matt observed Jilly enter the room and stop to speak to the maître d'. With a nod, the tuxedo-clad gentleman led the way toward the table.

Matt watched her head his way, and everything male in him snapped to attention. Her dark hair was pulled back in her familiar, professional chignon. A plain black, long sleeved, turtleneck dress hugged her body from her chin to just above her knees. Sheer black stockings, ending with strappy, black heels made her shapely legs appear endless. As far as he could tell, her jewelry consisted only of the small diamond studs twinkling on her earlobes. She looked understated, classy, and sexy as hell.

He drew a long, careful breath. How did she manage to look so cool yet so freakin' *hot* at the same time? And in a damn dress that showed absolutely no skin? But it was the *way* it showed no skin that had him shifting in his seat to relieve the discomfort in his groin. The dress clung to her just enough to offer a hint of her feminine curves. The sort of hint that made a man want to go exploring. The simplicity of the monochromatic style, her understated chignon, lent her a sophistication that left him aching to run his hands all over her and mess up all that cool perfection with some of the sexual heat scorching him.

Thanking the maître d' who held out the chair opposite Matt, she gracefully sat.

"Hi," she said, offering him a quick smile.

The fresh scent of clean laundry wafted toward him, befuddling what few brain cells hadn't drained from his head. Damn. When had the smell of newly washed clothes become so sensual? She'd left her glasses behind and highlighted her eyes with some sort of smoky color that made them appear even more huge and alluring than usual. His gaze dipped downward. Instead of emphasizing her full lips with a dark color, her mouth beckoned with nothing more than a glistening sheen of natural-colored gloss.

He swallowed. Hard. Yeah, she'd looked incredible walking toward him, but sitting across from him, close enough to touch, she made him forget his own damn name. It took a few seconds, but finally his inner voice chimed in, *Matt. Your name is Matt. I think. Now say hello before she thinks you belong in an institution.*

"Hi."

Looking around, she asked, "Where's Jack?"

"He canceled."

"Oh? Nothing's wrong, I hope."

"Wrong as in family emergency, or wrong as in did I screw up and scare him off?" The question came out harsher than he'd intended but, damn it, she had him completely off-center. And the fact that he appeared to be the only one unsettled irked him more than he cared to admit.

She shot him a look that clearly indicated she thought he was a pain in the ass. Well, good. If she thought that, maybe it would help cool some of the heat incinerating him.

"I meant family emergency, but since you're so prickly, maybe you *did* scare him off."

"No family emergency, nor did I scare him off. Apparently he met a woman at the indoor pool today, and they hit it off. While I was retrieving my cell phone earlier, the lady came into the bar. By the time I returned, Jack had decided that room service with her in his suite sounded better than dinner with us in the restaurant." He shrugged. "On the down side, it gives us less face time with him, but on the up side, it looks like he's having himself one hell of a good time this weekend, which can only reflect well on Maxximum."

She nodded. "I suppose you're right." Her gaze panned over the white linen-covered table, the gleaming crystal stemware, gold-rimmed china place setting, polished silverware, and crystal bowl filled with floating candles and red and white roses. Her gaze then shifted to the strings of tiny white holiday lights decorating the marble mantel and the low-burning fire, which cast the room in a subtle, golden glow, while soft music drifted down from unseen speakers. She was clearly observing what he'd already noticed—that the setting reflected romance and intimacy.

Their eyes met, and he was struck by how expressive those velvety, golden brown depths appeared. A man could easily get lost in those warm, intelligent, brandy-colored eyes. Her gaze searched his as if seeking the answer to some unanswered question. Was she wondering if he was thinking about the kiss they'd shared earlier? God knows he'd wondered if *she'd* been thinking about it. Much to his annoyance, he'd replayed that kiss in his mind about two hundred times already.

His gaze skimmed over her and he couldn't hold back the words. "You look gorgeous."

She blinked, then her lips twitched. "Why, thank you. But here's a little hint for future reference—that compliment would be so much more *complimentary* if you didn't sound so shocked when you said it."

Before he could assure her he was sincere, she asked, "Do you still want to have dinner? Just us?"

Hell, yes. He forced a nonchalant shrug in total contrast to the fire racing through him. "Might as well. We have to eat, and with Le Cabernet Bistro being a five-star restaurant, I'm guessing the food is reasonably decent."

"All right. Of course, I hope you're not too hungry. I recently found out that 'bistro' is French for 'a tiny, yet tasty portion that costs a lot more.'" She smiled and picked up her menu.

His heart thumped ridiculously at that smile. "You've also got chocolate-covered marshmallows—in case we're still hungry."

One eloquent brow hiked up. "What makes you think I'll share?"

"Because sharing is our lesson for today, and I'm certain you're an excellent student."

"Hmmm. That's odd. I thought our lesson for today was 'don't count your chocolate-covered marshmallows before they're hatched' and that you'd already learned it."

He winced. "Ouch. That hurt almost as much as that snowball to the chin I took." He gingerly moved his jaw back and forth.

She peered at his chin, then her eyes widened. "It does look a little red right here..." Reaching out, she brushed her fingertip over the spot with a feathery touch that stilled him. "I'm sorry. My aim was off."

"Really? What were you trying to hit—my eye?"

She laughed and pulled her hand away. "Of course not. Does it hurt?"

"Only when I inhale."

"I really am sorry."

He waved his hand in a dismissive gesture, surprised and more than a little annoyed to note that his hand wasn't quite steady. Damn it, his strong reaction to her bordered on the ridiculous. "Don't worry about it." He shot her a pointed stare. "*You* don't seem any worse for the wear from our altercation."

She smiled broadly. "Didn't get hit nearly as many times as you did."

The sommelier arrived at their table, saving Matt from thinking of a reply, which was just as well as it appeared that some valve had opened up in his neck, draining all the blood from his brain. And he knew exactly where all that blood had ended up—in his freakin' groin. Maybe having dinner alone with her hadn't been such a brilliant idea, but he couldn't back out now. And damn it, he didn't *want* to. He *wanted* to sit here. Wanted to look at her. Breathe in her unique scent. Study her fascinating eyes. And lips. Talk to her. Get to know her. Find out more about this woman who presented such an intriguing dichotomy of cool professionalism and heated sensuality—made all the more alluring because her sexiness was refreshingly understated. But he sure as hell wished he *didn't* want to do all those things. Nothing good could come of it. Yet he couldn't stop himself.

Following a brief discussion and consultation of the wine list, they ordered a Fontaine Vineyards chardonnay. After the sommelier left them, Jilly said, "This is great. We can sit here and drink wine until we really like each other. A couple dozen bottles ought to do it." Gracing him with a quick grin, she returned her attention to the menu.

Irritation slithered through Matt. Couple dozen bottles? Ha ha. Had he just thought her alluring? Fascinating? Surely he'd meant that she was a smartass and a thorn in his side. And how come *she* didn't appear to be having any problem at all ignoring him, while he felt hot and aroused and uncharacteristically flustered? And grumpier by the minute?

He'd always thought of himself as cool, detached, and in control. And he had been—until he'd found *her* in room 312 wearing her damn black satin lingerie. Until she'd loaned him her damn laptop. And fed him one of her damn chocolates. And kissed him in the damn snow. And worn a damn dress that fit her like smooth, black water poured on her curves.

Well, the hell with this. Sexual frustration definitely loved company, and he was tired of suffering alone. She couldn't possibly be as calm and collected as she clearly wanted him to believe. Yes, he was finished with her having the upper hand.

And it was about time he did something about it.

"I don't need to drink copious amounts of wine," he said softly. "I already like you." *But I sure as hell don't want to.*

Her gaze snapped up to his, and he noted with satisfaction that she appeared startled. And wary. A good start to toppling her from her aloof perch.

"And how much have you had to drink already?" she asked in a dry, skeptical voice.

"One beer." She'd taken the bait, now it was time to reel her in a bit. Not giving her time to question him further or regroup, he said, "So, tell me...are you attached?"

"Attached to what?"

Ah-ha! Avoiding the question by pretending not to understand. Excellent. "A man. Do you have a boyfriend?" No way could she pretend not to understand *that*. And based on her expression, the question clearly threw her off balance. Secure that he was once again strapped in the driver's seat, he leaned back and smiled.

But instead of answering, she asked a question of her own. "Why do you want to know if I have a boyfriend?"

He shrugged. "Just making conversation." *Oh, sure,* his inner voice piped in, dripping with sarcasm. *It's definitely not because you feel this overwhelming urge to know everything about her. Not because you want—make that* need—*to know if there's a man in her life.*

"No one steady. How about you—are you involved with anyone?"

"Define 'involved.'" Uh-oh. Now *he* was avoiding the question by pretending not to understand. How had she turned this around? Clearly he was a victim of one of those sneaky girl traps that unsuspecting guys fell into, only to find themselves swallowed whole before they knew what hit them.

"Do you have a steady girlfriend?"

"No." He debated whether or not to elaborate, but figured what the hell. If he hoped to learn more about her, it was only fair that he throw out a few tidbits himself. "I had a steady girlfriend, but we broke up last Christmas."

"Why?"

"I wanted to get married."

Her brows shot up. "And she didn't?"

"Oh, she did. But to my best friend."

Unmistakable sympathy filled her eyes and she set her menu aside. "That had to hurt."

A sheepish laugh escaped him. "Yeah, it definitely cut the jugular. Lost my girlfriend, my best friend and my job all in one fell swoop."

"Why your job?"

Again, he debated whether or not to tell her, but decided why not? He hadn't done anything wrong—except be too trusting. "We all worked together at Cutting Edge Advertising. The same day I discovered their affair, I also found out they'd stolen several of my ideas. Definitely not one of my better days."

"That's awful. What did you do?"

"I resigned."

Her eyes widened. "You didn't fight to get your ideas back?"

"No. Obviously that surprises you."

"Frankly, yes."

"I thought about it, believe me. But it would have amounted to my word against theirs and, at that point, I didn't want to involve myself in anything that would mean prolonged contact with either of them. So I cut my losses and left. After indulging in a week-long pity party, I couldn't stand myself anymore. So I picked myself up, stuck some Band-Aids on my bleeding wounds, and landed the job with Maxximum."

Jilly stared across the table at him, sympathy tugging on her heart. Unable to stop herself, she reached out and touched his hand. "I'm sorry, Matt. That's a terrible, hurtful thing for anyone to suffer through. Are you...still in love with her?"

"No." He looked down at her hand resting on his, and she followed his gaze. His skin felt warm and firm under her palm. Alarm bells clanged in her brain at how much she liked the look of her fingers resting against his and at how much she liked hearing that he didn't have a girl-friend.

Slipping her hand from his, she forced her gaze up and their eyes met. There was no mistaking the awareness that sizzled between them. He broke the spell by shaking his head. "I don't know why I told you all that."

She forced a smile. "I asked."

The sommelier appeared with their wine, and no sooner had he served them than the waiter materialized and requested their order. Jilly ordered the endive and Roquefort salad and the wood-smoked salmon entrée. Matt simply handed the waiter his unopened menu and said, "I'll have the same, please."

When the waiter left, Jilly reached for her wineglass and said, "Well, that explains a lot."

"What do you mean?"

"Getting so badly burned and betrayed by your past co-workers certainly explains why you hold everyone at Maxximum at arm's length. And leaving your old job under such circumstances, having to reestablish yourself all over again at a new firm, that certainly lends some perspective to your ambitiousness. I'd hate to be placed in such a difficult situation."

Silence stretched between them. Her gaze lowered, lingering over his broad chest, and she found herself wishing she were his cashmere sweater. He had pushed up his sleeves several inches, which revealed his strong forearms. A discreet gold watch encircled his wrist. And his hands...he had really nice hands. Long fingered, steady, and strong. They looked like they'd know how to stroke a woman.

Forcing her gaze back upward, she noted he was studying her in a very distracting way, as if trying to read her mind. Being the object of all that concentrated attention shot heat through her veins, and she suddenly wished she'd opted for a sleeveless dress that would let her skin release some of that heat. He looked about to say something when a series of soft beeps cut the silence.

She instantly noted how his shoulders tensed. He swiftly withdrew his cell phone from his pocket. After consulting the caller ID readout, he said, "I'm sorry. This is the call I've been expecting. Do you mind if I take it here?"

"Of course not. Would you like me to give you some privacy?"

"Not necessary. But thanks." He flipped open the phone and said, "Hi, Mom. Do you have the results?"

Jilly sipped her wine, trying not to listen, but with him sitting less than three feet away, it was impossible not to hear Matt's side of the conversation, even though he kept his voice low. Nor could she fail to notice the tension all but emanating from him, and his white-knuckle grip on the phone.

"What did the doctor say?" Closing his eyes, he dragged his hand down his face. Then he blew out a long breath as his posture relaxed. After several seconds of silence, he swallowed audibly. "Yeah, Mom, I'm here," he said, his voice rough with clear emotion. "Yes, it sure is great. The news we all wanted." He listened, then laughed. "What, me worried? Nah. I knew it all along.... We'll celebrate in style when you and Dad come into the city next weekend. How does the Rainbow Room sound? Stacey, Ray and the Barbie Queen are coming also.... We'll have a great time.... Yes, we'll definitely see the tree at Rockefeller Center...and all the shop windows along Fifth." He nodded a few times, then chuckled. "It's good to hear you laugh, too. Okay...tell them all I say hi. Yeah, this is going to be a great Christmas. I love you, Mom. Bye."

He flipped the phone shut with hands she noted weren't quite steady, but there was no mistaking the happy relief in his eyes. So *that* was the call he'd been expecting. Something unfamiliar squeezed inside Jilly at the realization that he'd obviously been very concerned about his mother. Between that and the story about the betrayal by his former fiancée and best friend, she was seized with the uncomfortable sensation that she'd misjudged this man.

"I couldn't help overhearing. It seems that was good news."

"Yes, thank God. A lump showed up on my mom's last mammogram. She's had to undergo a series of tests, and, well, for the last few weeks, suffice it to say, we've all been really worried. But she called to report that all her tests came back negative." His smile could have lit the entire room.

"That's wonderful. And I know how relieved you're feeling. My mom went through something similar two years ago. Luckily the lump was benign, but that space of time while we waited for the results..." She shuddered. "Awful. And so frightening."

"Exactly. I've been scared to death inside. My mom is so energetic and vital, the thought that she might have cancer..." He shook his head, then smiled. "But she doesn't." He lifted his glass. "A toast. To my mom—and yours. May they never scare us like that ever again."

Jilly laughed, then touched the rim of her glass to his. "I'll drink to that." After sipping her wine, she asked, "Your family is celebrating next weekend?"

"Yes. My parents, and my sister Stacey, her husband Ray, and my niece Rachel."

"Rachel is the Barbie Queen you mentioned?"

"She is. She's five and so adorable it's scary. You should see her. All big brown eyes and dark curly hair. And absolutely frighteningly brilliant."

She smiled. "Not that you're prejudiced."

"Not a bit. And, man, does she love Barbie. I can't wait to see her face on Christmas morning when she opens the Barbie Dream Mansion I bought her."

"*You* bought a Barbie Mansion? C'mon. You had someone else pick it out for you, right?"

He looked horrified. "And miss a chance to spend a few hours cavorting at the toy store? Are you nuts? I picked that mansion out myself, although if I'd known how much real estate and other goodies Barbie owns, I would have brought a mortgage broker along. That woman has *everything*. Boats, cars, campers, houses, horses, mansions, private jets, not to mention a very serious shoe fetish. After I was done in her aisle, I felt it was my manly duty to visit G.I. Joe and give him a head's-up as to what the deal was over on aisle ten. I told him, 'Dude, you need to ask this girl out.'"

She couldn't help but laugh. "Sounds like you and G.I. Joe had quite the bonding experience."

"Yeah, we're buds. But Rachel's excitement isn't going to come close to the surprise Stacey and I have planned for our folks. A ten-day cruise around the Caribbean. They've wanted to go for years, but have always put it off." His expression turned serious. "The last few weeks have been incredibly hard on all of us, but especially on Mom and Dad. They need and deserve a vacation."

"That's a great present."

"They're great parents."

He smiled, and Jilly smiled back. Something warm and fuzzy and more than a little scary seeped through her. Clearly there was more to Matt Davidson than the arrogant, brash competitor she'd spent the past year viewing him as. He was human. Had a disarming sense of humor. A family he clearly loved. He liked kids. Toy stores. He'd had his heart broken. And had lost his best friend. Liked chocolate-covered marshmallows. And had the sexiest smile she'd ever seen.

Realization slapped her like a wet towel to the face and her breath caught.

Oh, hell, she liked him.

She resisted the urge to thunk herself on the forehead. How stupid could she get, falling in *like* with the guy? Jeez. With all the technology out there, you'd think somebody could figure out a way to make her *dis*like him again. Bolstered from her conversation with Kate, she'd come to dinner determined to be cool and in control. But less than a half hour in, she was feeling all melty and warm and flustered.

"Well, now that you know more about me than you ever wanted to," he said, yanking her out of her reverie, "it's your turn." He leaned forward and lightly brushed his fingertips over the back of her hand, shooting pleasurable shivers up her arm. "How come someone so smart and talented and gorgeous, and who has such incredibly soft skin, doesn't have a boyfriend?"

She wanted, very much, to maintain her mantle of cool professionalism, but how could she hope to do so when the tingling feel and arousing sight of his fingers brushing over her hand melted her resolve like an ice cube tossed in boiling water? She should pull her hand away, she knew she should, but unable to resist the temptation of his touch, she instead shifted her hand a little closer to his. Unmistakable desire flared in his eyes, and he slowly explored her fingers with his own.

Forcing her mind to focus on his question, she said, "I don't have a steady boyfriend for several reasons, the biggest one being that I just don't have the time to devote to a relationship. All my energies are focused on my career and establishing myself at Maxximum, and it seems all the men I date grow to resent that—and harbor this annoying tendency to try to take charge of my life. Relationships, I've found, are like houseplants. If you don't give them a lot of time and attention, they wither up and die. Which is why I don't do well with houseplants, either. And besides that, it's simply been a while since I've met a man who genuinely interested me." *Hello—what about him?* her hormones screamed. *We're genuinely interested in him.*

Jilly wasn't sure if it was the wine, or the quiet understanding in his eyes, or the hypnotic brush of his fingers caressing her hand, or the fact that he'd given her some insight into himself and turn around was only fair, but the next thing she knew, she was telling him things she never thought she would. She talked about how her father had died of a heart attack at age thirty-six, leaving behind a sixteen-year-old Jilly and her thirty-five-year-old mother. How Dad's death had left her heartbroken, but had completely incapacitated her mother.

"She just couldn't cope," Jilly said quietly. "She'd loved him her whole life. They'd married right out of high school, and I came along pretty quickly. Dad was a mechanic—he could rebuild an entire engine with his eyes closed. They weren't rich, but he made a decent living, and my mom took to motherhood like a duck to water. Girl Scout leader, PTA, room mother, soccer mom, cooking, baking, crafts—she was a whiz at all that. But my dad took care of everything else, from the finances to the house maintenance. He always wanted to 'take care of his girls'...."

An image of her dad's smiling face flashed in her mind, bringing with it the same punch of loss that still hit her whenever she thought of him. "He was so great. So outgoing, and strong, and vital. When he died...God, I can't describe the mind-numbing shock."

"You don't have to," he said quietly, his gaze resting

on hers. He intertwined their fingers and gently squeezed. "I know exactly how it feels to have the rug jerked out from under you that way. In a blink, your whole world changes. Everything's gone. And you just feel...helpless."

"Exactly." The understanding and sympathy reflected in his serious gaze, the warmth of his hands clasping hers, rushed a heady combination of gratitude and heated awareness through her.

"What happened after your dad died?" he asked.

"Everything fell apart. Except for a part-time job waitressing during high school, my mother had never had a job outside the house. She'd never balanced a checkbook, made out the bills, mowed the lawn, changed the oil in the car, filed a tax return. She was the greatest mom on earth, but she was woefully unprepared for life without the safety net my dad had always provided by 'taking care' of us. And she was so bogged down in grief, she just couldn't cope."

"So you picked up the slack," he said, his gaze filled with dawning comprehension.

"I had no choice. We were long on bills and short on money. I took a job at a boutique in the mall, and Mom went back to waitressing. I learned how to use—and fix—the lawnmower, maintain the car, repair the plumbing, balance the checkbook—all of it." Jilly drew a deep breath, vividly recalling those lean, depressing, difficult years. "I promised myself I would never be placed in the same untenable position as my mom. I was determined to go to college, build a successful career, and have all the skills and knowledge I needed so that I wasn't dependant on anyone."

He smiled. "It would appear that you successfully met your goal."

She paused. Had she? To a certain degree, yes. She certainly didn't need anyone to take care of her. And her career was on the right track. But it suddenly occurred to her that she didn't have a partner to share her successes with. True, Jilly the ad executive was doing fine...but what about Jilly the woman?

Shoving the disturbing question aside, she said, "I've accomplished a great deal, but not the level of financial security I want. There's always another challenge to reach for."

"Like winning the ARC account."

She looked into his eyes and a fissure of understanding and awareness passed between them. "Yes."

Silence stretched for several seconds, then he asked, "How is your mom doing now?"

A smile pulled at Jilly's lips. "Great. It was a long, arduous road for her, but my college graduation proved a turning point for her. She enrolled at the local community college six years ago, squeezing in classes between her shifts at the restaurant. She only needs twelve more credits to earn her business degree—then watch out, world! I'm really proud of her."

"I bet she's proud of you, too."

"Well, she *is* my mom—that's her job."

The waiter arrived with their salads. Matt slowly released her hands, and she instantly missed the intimacy of his warm skin, the feel of his fingers gliding over hers. She blinked, feeling as if she were emerging from a cozy, intimate cocoon where she and Matt had somehow connected, whispering secrets like lovers in the dark.

The heat simmering in his gaze made the soles of her feet sweat and had her shifting in her seat. She glanced down at the salad the waiter had placed before her.

Damn it, she didn't want salad. She wanted *him*. Naked. Aroused. Hot. Inside her.

The image barreled into her mind, knocking everything else aside. Fire whooshed through her, hardening her nipples.

"You okay?" he asked.

"I'm...fine." Damn it, he was looking at her in the most disconcerting way—as if he knew exactly what she was thinking. But he didn't look smug about it. No, his expression appeared to say, *Yeah, me too—and what the hell are we going to do about it?*

Since she didn't know the answer to that question, Jilly picked up her fork, stabbed an endive and steered the conversation to the less personal topic of the madhouse Manhattan turned into during the holidays. Matt picked up the conversational life ring she tossed, and she laughed at his story of staggering down Fifth Avenue under the weight of a Barbie Dream Mansion housed in a box nearly as big as him.

During their entrée, Matt revealed he was a die-hard Mets fan, and as Jilly was a die-hard Yankees fan, a lively debate ensued, a friendly dispute that grew more animated over after-dinner cappuccinos when it came to light that Matt's hockey team was the Rangers, while Jilly rooted for the Islanders.

"Looks like we'll just have to agree to disagree," Jilly finally said with a laugh, setting her empty china cup on its gold-rimmed saucer. "We definitely don't have much in common." Yet be that as it may, she couldn't recall the last time she'd enjoyed a date so much.

That stopped her like she'd walked into a cement wall. Date? Oh, no. Panic fluttered in her, wiping away her amusement like a wet mop over a dirty floor. This was *not* a date. This was sharing a meal with a business associate. Big difference.

Yeah, but it sure felt like a date. She mentally ticked off the signs—romantic setting, soft background music, candlelight, wine, delicious meal, stimulating conversation, sexy man sitting across from her, sexual awareness humming between her and that man. Yup, this had all the earmarks of a date. A really fun, enjoyable date. A really fun, enjoyable date that was about to end, leaving them both bound for room 312.

Matt studied her for several long seconds over the rim of his own cup before setting it down, and Jilly's heart skipped a beat at the sudden intense, compelling look in his eyes. Leaning forward, he said, "Actually, I think we have quite a bit in common."

Uh-oh. Somehow, in the last few seconds, the light mood that had pervaded their meal shifted, and all the simmering tension she'd managed—almost—to ignore during dinner smacked her in the face. Striving to appear outwardly calm, she asked, "Quite a bit in common? What makes you say that?"

For an answer, he reached out and lightly clasped her wrists, shooting heated tingles through her veins. "The fact that your pulse is racing...just like mine. The fact that even though we agreed we would, you can't forget the kiss we shared...just like me. The fact that I'm very attracted to you...as I think you are to me."

Oh, boy, this conversation *had* taken a detour. And down a very unsafe road. She couldn't deny she wanted him, but neither could she ignore how foolhardy it would be to give in to that want. She wished she could label his statements arrogant and conceited but, damn it, all she could call them was correct. And she had to give him credit for facing head-on this...whatever it was between them. The coward in her would have voted for avoiding it like a bad rash. In fact, that was an excellent idea.

Offering what she hoped passed for a carefree smile, she said, "You're a good-looking, personable man. I think it's safe to say that most women would find you attractive."

"Thank you. But that's not what I meant. There's something more going on here. God knows I don't want to feel this heat that's crackling between us. I've been trying my damnedest to ignore it, but I can't ignore something that's hitting me in the face like an open-handed slap." His serious gaze searched her. "You feel it, too."

More than anything, she wanted to deny it, but how could she utter such a blatant lie—especially in light of his honesty? Even if she managed to push the words past her lips, an Academy Award winner she was not. He'd know in a heartbeat she was nothing but a big fat liar.

"I feel it," she admitted. "But I'm not happy about it."

"You don't see me jumping up and down and calling for the champagne. Question is, what are we going to do about it?"

"I don't know. What are the choices?"

"Seems to me there're only two. We can try to ignore it—"

"Which is definitely the smart choice."

"Smart, yes. But possible? Not likely."

Her heart slapped against her ribs so hard, he surely had to hear it. "I'd think that someone who's been so badly burned in the past would run—not walk—away from another interoffice romance."

"Believe me, it's the *last* thing I thought I'd ever consider. But that leads me to choice two."

"Which is...?"

"Spend the rest of this weekend exploring this spark between us, then going our separate ways."

She looked into his serious, dark blue eyes, and her breath caught. "You mean indulge in an affair here at the resort, but come Tuesday back at the office, it's business as usual."

"Exactly."

It was so tempting. *He* was so tempting. Still, her common sense raised its hand and compelled her to ask, "Don't you think the fact that we've known each other in the biblical sense will be distracting and awkward at work?"

"I'm sure it will be." He reached out and gently ran his fingertip down her cheek. "But between this attraction and only one of us being able to win the ARC account, it's going to be distracting and awkward anyway."

"In other words, if we're going to feel 99 percent awkward anyway, what's the difference if we feel 99.9 percent awkward?"

"Right. So why not satisfy our lust this weekend only, then never speak of this 'at the winery' incident again?"

Something tickled her memory, and a frown pulled down her brows. Those words sounded suspiciously familiar. Before she could think on it further, he lifted her hand and pressed a warm kiss against her palm.

"I think it's the perfect solution to a mutual attraction neither of us wants, but that neither of us can ignore," he said softly, his warm breath beating against her palm, his gaze steady and intense. "So, whaddaya say? Wanna sleep with me...Rusty?"

7

JILLY ACTUALLY FELT ALL the blood drain from her face. Her eyes goggled and she stared at him, horrified, mortified. *Oh. My. God.*

Clearly he'd overheard at least the tail end of her conversation with Kate. Snatches of Jilly's words reverberated through her brain...*the sort of kiss you'd like to have last for three weeks...I want to do a hell of a lot more than just kiss him...we'll satisfy our lust this weekend only, then never speak of this 'at the winery' incident again...I haven't had sex in so long, you could nickname me Rusty.*

With a moan, she plopped her elbows on the table, then lowered her face into her hands. She didn't know who the Patron Saint of Potholes was, but she offered up a prayer anyway, begging for a large cavity to yawn open in the floor and swallow her.

"How much did you hear?" she finally asked in a small voice.

He touched his fingertips under her chin until she raised her head to look at him. "Enough to know that you want me, which works out well because I sure as hell want you. And enough to know that it's been a while for you, which again works out well because it's been a while for me, too. I've never been so powerfully attracted to a woman in my life. As far as I'm concerned, there isn't a decision to make. So, it's up to you...."

His words, spoken in that low, husky voice, flicked fire

over her, extinguishing her embarrassment. He'd served the ball into her court. He wanted her. Now she needed to decide if she was going to return his serve, or pack up her gear and hit the locker rooms—a decision that took all of five seconds. Actually he was right—there wasn't any decision to make. The whispers of common sense were drowned out by the screams of her body telling her to make love with him.

Nine months, three weeks and nineteen days was enough.

She blew out a long breath. "I'd be willing to wager that my sexual drought has been longer than yours."

"Then let's end the dry spell." He trailed his fingertips along her jaw. A delicate shiver of delight trembled across her shoulders at the touch, and his eyes darkened at her response. "There's definitely a spark between us, Jilly."

"That's my brain shorting out. This proposition of yours— I must admit, you've aroused my interest."

"You've aroused a lot more than that. And just by sitting there."

"Hmmm. Imagine what might happen if I put a little effort into it."

"I *have* been imagining it. Constantly." His gaze dropped to her mouth and feminine satisfaction surged through her at his low groan. Leaning toward her, he whispered, "I really like your lips."

With the decision made, she didn't attempt to hold back the desire and need and anticipation pumping hot through her veins. She reached out and whispered the tip of her index finger over his mouth. "I really like your lips, too. Would you like me to show you how much?"

The fire in his gaze scorched her. He grasped her hand and pressed a kiss in the center of her palm. "Oh, yeah."

"Let's go."

Since they'd already signed the check, charging their meals to the room, they stood. Matt held out his hand. Without hesitation Jilly entwined her fingers with his, and they left the restaurant.

They crossed the lobby, and it was all Jilly could do not to give in to the urge to run across the pale marble floor, dragging him along in her haste. Her hands positively itched with the need to touch him. Her skin felt tight and hot, and she couldn't wait to get this dress off her. And his hands on her. She toyed with the idea of pulling him into an alcove and kissing him until they couldn't breathe. But she knew that once they started, there'd be no stopping, so starting in a public place was not a good idea.

As they neared the elevators, she asked, "What's our condom situation?"

"Under control."

Thank God. Because at the moment, it was about the only thing that was. She couldn't recall ever feeling so impatient for a man's touch. To feel his skin against hers. Taste his lips.

Just play it cool 'til you get to the room, her inner voice said soothingly. Yeah, she could do that.

The instant the elevator doors enclosed them in privacy, however, he yanked her against him, and all thoughts of cool were incinerated by his fiery kiss. His tongue explored her mouth while his strong hands streaked down her back, molding her closer. She arched into him, reveling in the feel of his erection pressing against her belly. Plunging her fingers through his thick hair, she savored the silky heat of his mouth.

The doors opened, and still wrapped around each other, alternately kissing and laughing, they headed awkwardly down the corridor to their room. Matt reached into his pants pocket and frowned. After a quick pat-down of his other pockets, he said, nipping his way across her jawline, "I don't have my key. Must have forgotten it when I came back for my phone earlier."

"I have mine." At the door Jilly turned away from him and fumbled impatiently in her purse. Standing behind her, Matt wrapped his arms around her waist and gently bit the side of her neck.

Her eyes glazed over. "That's not helping me find my key," she said in a shaky voice.

"You need to be more careful and keep your key at the ready," he whispered against her ear, his warm breath showering shivers of delight through her. "You never know who might be lurking about."

"This seemed like a pretty safe hallway—till now."

"Exactly. What if someone came up behind you?" His arms tightened around her waist, and she leaned back against his long, muscular body, absorbing his heat, reveling in the tensile strength of those arms, and the press of his erection against her buttocks.

Turning her head, she nipped her teeth against his jaw. "I guess they'd get me."

An agonized groan rumbled in his throat. "I can't wait."

"You can't be any more anxious than me. I have nine months, three weeks and nineteen days to make up for."

"You're kidding."

"I'm not."

He nuzzled her neck. "Well, I'm at your disposal and more than happy to help. Have you found the key yet?"

Her fingers closed over the plastic key card. "Got it. Listen, is hard and fast all right with you for the first time?"

He pressed his erection tighter against her buttocks and slid one hand up to cup her breast, eliciting a gasp from her. "You even need to ask? If you don't hurry up and open the door, hard and fast is going to happen right here in the hall."

She yanked the key from her small, beaded bag, then jammed the card into the slot. Matt followed her into the room. The instant the door clicked shut, all bets were off. Splaying her hands against his chest, she backed him against the wall. His mouth came down on hers in a hot, wild, openmouthed kiss at the same time his impatient fingers undid her chignon and then plunged his hands into the loosened locks. She moaned, and arched against him, rubbing her pelvis against his erection while his hands skimmed over her hips, urging her closer.

Impatience and fire raced through her. Feeling like a volcano on the verge of eruption, she shoved her hands under his cashmere sweater, smoothing her palms up his ridged abdomen. Breaking off their kiss, she tugged the soft wool upward. "Off."

While he yanked the sweater over his head, she retreated one step and applied herself to the zipper on the back of her dress.

After he toed off his shoes and yanked off his socks, he set his hands on her shoulders and turned her around. "Let me," he said in a harsh rasp. He lowered the zipper with a quick, fluid tug. Turning her to face him, he slid the material down her body, the sleek texture abrading her oversensitive, aroused skin. Releasing the dress, the silk puddled at her feet, leaving her clad in her lacy black bra, wisp-of-satin black panties, lace-topped thigh-high stockings and her heels. Breathing choppy, heart rapping against her ribs with rapid-fire beats, she reached for his belt.

He turned them so that her back now pressed against the wall. His mouth captured hers in another deep, tongue-dancing, frantic kiss. While she battled his stubborn belt buckle with clumsy, impatient fingers, he flicked open the front clasp of her bra and filled his hands with her aching breasts, teasing her already rigid nipples until she thought she'd scream. He left her lips and blazed hot, openmouthed kisses down her neck, then bent his head to draw her taut nipple into the wet heat of his mouth.

A gasp of delight escaped her, and temporarily abandoning his belt, she dropped her head back against the wall, and tunneled her fingers into his silky hair. Arching upward, she urged him to take more, and he obliged, his tongue and teeth and lips worshiping her breasts until her thighs trembled, and the musky scent of her feminine arousal rose between them from her damp flesh.

With a low, guttural growl his hands skimmed along her sides, pushing her panties down her legs until she impatiently kicked them aside. And then his mouth was again on hers, stealing her breath. She clung to his shoulders, and her need rising to the point of desperation, she lifted one leg and hooked it around his hips. One strong, masculine hand cupped her buttocks while the other slipped between her thighs. When his fingers slid over her aching, wet feminine folds, they both groaned.

"Jilly..." His ragged breaths beat against her lips.

Need—razor sharp and demanding—seized her and she spread her legs wider. "Now," she ground out. "*Now.*"

His fingers slid inside her, and she gasped. Her orgasm rocketed through her, ripping a low, husky *oooohhh* from her throat. She arched her back, reveling in the knee-weakening shudders consuming her.

When her spasms subsided, she limply clung to him, biting her lip against the pleasurable aftershocks rippling through her as he continued slowly to stroke her.

"Wow." Leaning forward, she lightly nipped the side of his neck. "Thanks, I needed that."

"My pleasure."

"Actually, it was mine. *Now* it's your turn."

"Can't wait."

With his body on the verge of detonation, Matt scooped her up in his arms and carried her to the bed where he set her on the comforter with a gentle bounce. She reached up for him, but he backed away, muttering, "Condom," simultaneously blessing the fact that he had some, and cursing the fact that they were in his damn overnight bag. Turning away from her for even an instant required an almost Herculean effort.

Dropping to his knees, he pawed through his bag, heedless of the mess he was making of his clothing. Light suddenly flooded the room and without taking the time to look up, he said, "Thanks."

Damn it, where were the condoms? He tossed underwear, T-shirts, sweaters and socks over his shoulder. Just as panic was about to set in, he located them in a side pocket. He grabbed one and stood, then turned toward the bed. And stilled.

Jilly lay sprawled on the bedspread, her dark hair, mussed from his hands, spread around her head like a halo, an image not at all in keeping with the rest of her, which was the personification of sin. Legs splayed, wearing nothing save those lacy thigh-high sheer black stockings, she leaned up on her elbows and regarded him through smoky eyes.

His gaze wandered downward, taking in her lush mouth, flushed skin, and erect nipples, then lower, over the feminine curve of her hips and the triangle of dark curls at the apex of her shapely legs. He inhaled sharply and the delicate scent of female arousal inundated his senses, spiking his temperature several degrees. She looked like she'd just stepped from the pages of a book entitled *Matt's Every Fantasy.*

"Listen," she said in a husky rasp, "you took the edge off, and as much as I appreciate it, I still feel like a bottle rocket about to go off. If you're just going to stand there, I might have to go see what the guy in room 311 is doing."

"Like hell," he said with a growl. Tossing the condom onto the bedspread, he applied himself to his belt. "I hope hard and fast is still okay with you 'cause I don't think I'm gonna last much longer."

She shot him a sexy smile that shaved away a few more seconds of whatever time he had left before he exploded. "Hard and fast sounds perfect."

He stripped off his pants and boxers in one swift movement. Unmistakable appreciation gleamed in her eyes as her gaze riveted on his straining erection. He started to reach for the condom, but halted when she crawled to the edge of the bed, like a sleek cat stalking toward a bowl of cream, then rose to her knees in front of him.

She reached out and stroked her fingers down his aroused length, causing him to suck in a sharp breath. His fingers roamed up and down her back while he watched her slide her hands over him, gently cupping and squeezing him. He withstood the sweet torture of her caresses as long as he could, then, with his vision glazed with need, he gently grasped her wrist. "Can't take any more," he rasped, reaching for the condom.

After sheathing himself, he leaned over her, pressing

her back into the mattress. Their mouths met in a wild mating of lips and tongues as he sank into her velvety, wet heat. White-hot need pounded through his every nerve ending, stripping him of all semblance of control. His world narrowed to the heated place where his body was intimately joined with hers, stroking, thrusting, at an ever maddening pace. He gritted his teeth and tried to hold off his rapidly approaching orgasm, but when she moaned, "Matt..." against his mouth, the battle was lost. Burying his face against her silky, smooth neck, a long groan rattled in his throat and his release shuddered through him.

He wasn't certain how long he remained still buried in her snug heat, breathing in her delicate scent, his heart rapping against his ribs, his mind fogged over, before she nudge him gently with her hip.

"Can't take a deep breath," she whispered.

He pushed up his torso, propping his weight on his palms, and looked down into her flushed face. Their gazes met. Damn, she looked as blown away as he felt. Two words reverberated through the brain this woman had just turned to mush: Man Overboard!

Brushing a damp curl from her smooth cheek, he said, "I want you to know that I, uh, usually have a little more finesse than that."

"No complaints here," she assured him. A smile tugged up one corner of her delicious mouth and she stretched beneath him like a contented cat. "Although I look forward to you proving that. And thanks for the compliment. Nice to know that I made you lose control."

"Sweetheart, you made me lose my mind." He lowered his head and ran his tongue over her plump lower lip. "Definitely the next time you've gone nine months, three weeks and nineteen days without sex and you're needing a little pick-me-up, I hope you'll call me."

"Well, it's been about five minutes..."

He chuckled. "'Fraid I'm going to need a bit longer to recover."

She tickled her fingers down his back and over his buttocks. "Unless you keep doing that," he amended, nipping and kissing along her jawline. "That will definitely speed up the recovery period."

"Hmmmm," she murmured, continuing her stroking. "Speeding up the recovery period sounds good to me. I have a lot of time to make up for, and now that I know how...enthusiastic you are, I really would hate to have to seek out the guy in room 311."

Matt stilled as an unpleasant sensation that felt distinctly like jealousy washed over him. She was kidding, of course, but the mere thought of another man touching her just flat-out pissed him off. *Yo, Matt, buddy, that's not good. 'Cause after this weekend, other guys are gonna be touching her—and you won't be.*

He inwardly scowled at his inner voice. Yeah, well, she was *his* for the rest of the weekend, and he fully intended to make the most of it.

"Now that we've explored the benefits of hard and fast," he said, studying her eyes, "I suggest we move on to slow and easy."

"Put me in, coach. What did you have in mind?"

"You. Me. A shower. Then maybe you'd like a massage?"

"Depends on who's giving the massage—you, or some muscle-bound guy named Sven at the resort's spa?"

He cocked a brow. "Who would you prefer?"

"You," she said without hesitation.

"Then come with me."

She smiled. "That's the best offer I've had in nine months, three weeks and nineteen days."

JILLY STOOD IN THE SHOWER, warm water sluicing over her, and locked her knees to keep her legs from collapsing like overcooked noodles.

"Magic hands," she murmured, as his soapy palms slowly massaged their way down her back. "You have magic, sinful hands."

His arms came around her from behind, and he drew her gently back against him, nestling his erection against her buttocks. While his lips nuzzled the vulnerable spot behind her ear, his hands roamed slowly over her, drawing drugging circles around her nipples, then wandered lower, over her abdomen. When his fingers slid between her thighs and slicked over her sensitive feminine folds, a long, low purr vibrated in her throat.

"I have a confession to make," he whispered against her ear. "I wondered what you looked like under those prim, proper suits you wear."

A zing of feminine satisfaction raced through her. "And now that you know?"

He slipped a finger inside her while his other hand played over her hardened nipples, dragging another long moan from her. "I figured you'd be beautiful. But I hadn't guessed you'd be so...uninhibited."

"Is that a complaint?"

"God, no. I admire a woman who knows what she wants and isn't afraid to ask for it."

"Really?"

"Really."

"Well, that's very good news." She turned in his arms, sifted her fingers through his wet hair, and rubbed herself against his erection. "Because I want you to make love to me again. Slow and easy. Right now."

His eyes darkened. Guiding them both fully under the warm spray of water, he rinsed the soap from their bodies, then pressed her back against the tiles. The cool ceramic against her shoulders provided a stunning contrast to the heat coursing through her.

"I have a confession to make as well," she murmured as his hands meandered down her wet body. "This morning, when I saw you draped in a towel, my heart performed these crazy little flip-flops. But now—" she allowed her gaze to linger pointedly on his impressive erection "—my heart is about to call it quits. Seeing you naked definitely dispels the theory that all men are created equal."

He smiled and hooked one hand under her knee, raising her leg to settle over his hip, while the fingers of his other hand slowly caressed between her thighs. "Did you know that your eyes have little green flecks in them?" he asked. "And that they turn this incredible smoky color when you're aroused?"

"I knew about the green flecks, but not about the smokiness." A pleasure-filled moan escaped her. "Guess that means they're smoky right now, huh?"

"Yeah. You ready for slow and easy?"

"Actually, I'm not sure how much more slow and easy I can stand, but bring it on."

"My pleasure." Lowering her leg, he kissed and nuzzled his way with excruciating, maddening leisure down her body. Pressing her palms against the tiles, Jilly simply gave herself over to his slow, deliberate seduction, succumbing to the feel of his strong hands and gentle mouth skimming over her. He sank to his knees, his sorcerer's fingers massaging first one leg, then the other, while his lips and tongue glided over her belly.

Long moans purred in her throat when he replaced his hands with his mouth and slowly licked and kissed his way up her leg, awakening every inch of her skin. Forcing her heavy eyelids open, her avid gaze riveted on the erotic sight of Matt on his knees before her, his dark head between her legs, his tongue tracing a trail up her inner thigh.

At the first touch of his tongue to her feminine folds, she gasped. He slipped his hands beneath her buttocks, urging her closer, his lips and tongue tasting, licking, kissing, making love to her with his mouth until she was mindless with need. Grasping his shoulders, the dam of tension he'd built in her burst, and her orgasm throbbed through her.

Her eyes slid shut, and she pressed back against the tiles in an effort to remain upright, quivering with pleasure, feeling like a bowl of warm, melted chocolate. Her mind registered the familiar sound of a condom wrapper tearing open. Deciding this warranted further investigation, she forced her eyelids open just in time to see Matt slip on a condom. With the warm water bouncing off his broad shoulders, he grasped her hips and lifted her. Clinging to his shoulders, she wrapped her legs around his hips, and with his compelling gaze intent upon hers, he slipped into her body in a single stroke.

"Oh, my," she breathed.

Tangling her hands in his wet hair, she pulled his face to hers for a deep kiss. The taste of her feminine musk, mixed with his own delicious taste, inundated her senses.

He caressed her with long, leisurely, deep strokes, withdrawing nearly all the way from her body, then slowly filling her again. She absorbed every thrust, every exquisite sensation washing through her. The tension coiled within her once again, and her body tightened, a reaction he clearly felt for he whispered against her lips, "Ready for more?"

She arched against him. "Yes. More."

His strokes lengthened, quickened. Harder, faster. Deeper. "Now," he rasped. "Come with me, now."

Her eyes slid shut, and a growl of pure pleasure poured from her lips as her body throbbed in unison with his.

When the tremors finally subsided, a sensation of utter languor stole through her, loosening her limbs.

He gently released her, then after a quick rinse under the soothing, warm spray, he turned off the faucet. Slipping a thick, fluffy white towel from the chrome rack just outside the shower, he dried her with the soft terry cloth, then gently blotted the water from her hair. After scooping her up in his arms—a good thing since someone had stolen the bones from her body—he carried her to the bed where he set her down, then settled himself on his side next to her. Replete, sated, and more relaxed than she could ever before recall feeling, she turned toward him, slipped her leg between his, and snuggled against his chest, experiencing the same delightful cocoon of warmth as she had last night during those brief seconds before she'd fully wakened. His rapid heartbeat thumped intimately against her cheek. She inhaled, and the musky scent they'd created together filled her head.

"You're really good at that," she murmured, her lips brushing against his broad chest.

"Thank you, and right back atcha." He brushed a kiss over her hair. "But here's a little hint for future reference—that compliment would be so much more *compli-*

mentary if you didn't sound so shocked when you said it."

She chuckled at his use of her earlier words to him. "Not shocked. Actually not even surprised." Yet, no sooner had she said the words, than she realized she *had* been surprised—though not about Matt's skills in bed. There'd been little doubt in her mind that making love with Matt would be good. But she hadn't expected it to be like...this. So intense. Mind blowing. Hadn't anticipated it making her feel so vulnerable. Hadn't counted on him being so generous. So tender. Hadn't considered that sharing their bodies would result in her feeling anything more than physical release. But the warm fuzzies tapping on her heart made it clear that she should have considered that.

His fingers touched under her chin, and she lifted her face. Their eyes met, and her breath caught at his serious expression. Her common sense demanded that she toss out a flip comment, a lighthearted quip, but no words formed in her mind.

"Do you know how beautiful you are?" he asked softly.

The husky timbre of his voice, the compelling way he was looking at her, the gentle brush of his fingertips against her skin as he tucked a stray curl behind her ear, all conspired to render her speechless.

"The way you look," he continued, his fingers tracing hypnotically over her face, "your scent, the way you taste...all beautiful."

"Th-thank you." Whew. Good thing she was already lying down or she would have slithered to the floor. Forcing a light note into her voice, she said, "You're not so bad yourself."

His serious expression cleared, and he smiled. "I have a confession to make. I'm hungry."

"*Already?* That was quick."

He laughed. "I mean for food...first. I some need sustenance to refuel before we begin round three."

"Are you thinking room service?"

"Not exactly."

His innocent expression instantly raised her suspicions. She narrowed her eyes at him. "You're angling to get some of my chocolate-covered marshmallows."

She had to press her lips together to contain her amusement at his exaggerated look of shock.

"*Moi?*" he asked, eyes wide. "I would never stoop so low as to angle. Of course, if you were to *offer* one—so I shouldn't expire from sex-induced hunger—I probably wouldn't refuse."

"Uh-huh." She tapped her finger against the center of his chest. "You know what I think? I think my chocolate-covered marshmallows are all you're after."

"Wrong. I'm after your chocolate-covered marshmallows *and* your body." A speculative gleam sparkled in his eyes, and he trailed his index finger slowly down her body, igniting tiny bonfires on her skin. "And if we actually placed the chocolate-covered marshmallows *on* your body, in a connect-the-dots sort of way...well, no telling what might happen then. Whaddaya say?"

"I say you've got yourself a snack."

8

MATT AWOKE TO A SHAFT of early-morning light gilding the room. His senses all engaged simultaneously, all of them registering the same thing: Jilly.

Jilly's warm body sprawled across his as he lay on his back. The feel of Jilly's hand resting on his chest, directly over the spot where his heart beat. The soft curve of Jilly's hip beneath his palm. The sensation of Jilly's shapely thigh hooked over his legs. Jilly's unique scent, spiced with the heady musk of their spent passion. Jilly's round, coral-tipped breasts pressed against his side. Jilly's warm breath blowing gently over his ribs. Jilly's shiny tangle of hair spread across his torso.

He rubbed one of those midnight curls between his thumb and forefinger, instantly recalling an image of his hands tunneled through those lustrous strands, his erection buried deep in her body, his name sighing from her lips as they shared another round of heart-stopping lovemaking.

Heart stopping. That's exactly what it had been. Intense. Incredible. In a way he couldn't describe, because it was completely unfamiliar. He felt like he'd just parachuted down into a foreign country without benefit of so much as a freakin' map.

It was as if everything he'd ever felt for a woman before was suddenly magnified a hundredfold, rendering every woman who'd come before Jilly pale in comparison. It was one thing to be turned on by her but, hell, he hadn't expected to be *so* turned on. Or so enthralled by her touch. Or so captivated by her smile. Attracted to her sense of humor and fierce need for independence. Fascinated by the flashes of mischief in her eyes. Damn it, he just hadn't expected to be so completely captured by everything about her.

Where were all these unwanted...feelings coming from? He liked her. Admired her. Wanted to learn all about her. In and out of bed.

He drew a deep breath. Oh, man. This was bad. *Really* bad. Definitely not the way this weekend was supposed to go down. He and Jilly were supposed to share a few laughs, a few orgasms, then—*badda-bing*—back to work as usual.

Well, one night in her arms left him no doubt that there was no chance in hell of *that* happening because there was no way he'd be able to put this weekend behind him and pretend it hadn't happened. Not when the taste of her, the feel and scent of her, the sound of her moaning his name as she found her release in his arms, were all permanently etched in his mind.

You're an idiot, his pain-in-the-ass inner voice said, in a disgusted tone. *You never should have slept with her.*

Great. *Now* you tell me.

Hey, I tried to tell you before you hit the sheets that this had "mistake of Godzilla-size proportions" tattooed all over it, his inner voice interjected. *But did you listen to me, Hormone-Man? Nooooo. You let this chick get your boxers all in a wad and now you've started something that will land you right back in the same mess you found yourself in with Tricia—sleeping with the enemy.*

He squeezed his eyes shut and banished the voice. Okay, indulging in sex with Jilly hadn't been smart, especially since he had the uncomfortable feeling that something much more significant than just sex had passed between them. But he wouldn't make the same mistakes he'd made with Tricia. No way. Forewarned was forearmed. This time he knew going in that the woman he was dealing with was ambitious and badly wanted the same account he did.

Yeah, but now he also knew how soft her skin was. Knew her delicious taste. The silky texture of her hair. How incredible it felt to be buried deep in her velvety warmth. That was the sort of knowledge that could cloud his judgment. Cost him his competitive edge. And maybe a hell of a lot more.

But only if he let it. And he wouldn't. So he liked her. So he was attracted to her. Big deal. As long as he didn't do something stupid like fall in love with her, everything would be fine. He was in control.

Feeling considerably cheered by his mental pep talk, he skimmed his hand over the silky curve of her waist. She stirred in his arms, then lifted her head, and looked at him through eyes heavy-lidded with the remnants of sleep. A slow smile curved her lips. "Good morning."

Two words and a smile. That's all it took to sucker-punch all his fine control into next week.

"Good morning."

Stacking her hands on his chest, she rested her chin on her fingers and looked at him through solemn eyes. "We have a big problem here, Matt."

Damn. She felt their connection, too. That just complicated things further. And surely should have filled him with wariness, as opposed to this sensation that felt suspiciously like relief. With a dose of happiness thrown in for good measure.

"Look, Jilly, I—"

"Because I don't smell coffee."

He stared at her. "Huh?"

"Coffee. I distinctly recall us agreeing at some point last night that whoever woke up first was in charge of rounding up the coffee—preferably in an IV drip. Since you were looking at me when I opened my eyes just now, you obviously awoke first. But I don't smell coffee. So you're in big trouble."

His hands slid down her smooth back to the deliciously warm curve of her buttocks. "Oh, yeah? What kind of trouble?"

"As in you owe me big time."

"Are we talkin' money here? How much?"

"Money?" she scoffed. "Oh, no." She shifted, and ran her hand down his abdomen, brushing her fingers over the tip of his erection. "I demand a flesh payment."

"And if I refuse to give in to your heinous demands?"

For an answer, she rolled off him and rose from the bed. His gaze stalked her gorgeous, naked form as she strolled out of his line of vision with a sinful sway of her hips. He heard the sounds of her readying the room's coffeemaker, which was situated on a shelf just outside the bathroom. The ripping of the plastic bag, then the pouring of the grounds into the filter. Filling the glass pot, adding the water to the machine, then flipping the switch. Seconds later she appeared and, leaning against the wall, dangled a white ceramic cup from her index finger.

"If you choose not to give in to my heinous demands, I won't share my freshly brewing coffee with you," she said.

Without taking his gaze from her, he rose from the bed and walked slowly toward her. "You drive a hard bargain, Jilly."

Her gaze dipped down to his erection. "A topic you're familiar with, I see."

When he reached her, he plucked the cup from her fingers, tossed it onto the bed, then yanked her into his arms. Their lips met in a lush, intimate kiss that shot fire through his veins.

"All right," he said, dragging his mouth down her soft neck. "I'll pay up this time, but only because I'm desperate for that coffee."

Her hand slipped between them. She wrapped her fingers around his aroused length and he sucked in a sharp breath.

"Hmmmm. Are you *sure* coffee is what you want, Matt?"

"Yeah." Dipping his knees, he picked her up and carried her back to the bed. "But I want you first."

AN HOUR LATER, Jilly stepped from the shower and wrapped one of the resort's fluffy white towels around her, sarong style. Freshly showered, and relaxed, she was ready to face the day. No doubt about it, nothing like a good bout—or several good bouts—of sex to put a spring in the step.

And as long as she remembered that that's all this was—just sex—everything would be fine. And she'd do it even if the effort to remember killed her. She wouldn't dwell on the intensity of their lovemaking. She'd forget about the heavenly texture of his skin beneath her hands and mouth. Push aside the memory of him filling her, touching her everywhere, murmuring her name like a prayer. Bludgeon all recollection of them laughing together while they fed each other chocolate-covered marshmallows. Yup, she had everything in perspective and she was in control.

After exiting the bathroom, she rounded the corner and saw Matt standing next to the phone. Matt wearing nothing except his boxer briefs—which raised her temperature—and a decidedly guilty look—which raised her curiosity.

"Something wrong?" she asked.

"Nope."

"You sure?"

"Yup."

"Were you able to reach Jack?"

"Just got off the phone with him. Looks like we're on our own for today."

She raised her brows. "What is he doing?"

"He's driving out to Orient Point with his new lady friend, Carol. They'll be gone all day, but Jack said he'd meet us for dinner here at the resort at seven."

She blew out a long breath. "Well, that puts us in a rather awkward position. Dinner last night was one thing, but Adam isn't going to be too happy to learn that so much of Maxximum's schmooze time is being stolen away by Jack's new friend."

"Well, short of kidnapping Jack, there isn't much we can do about it. Besides, it might work out for the best. Jack told me him and Carol are getting along like gangbusters." He shot her a pointed look. "I told him I understood completely."

Warmth flooded her at the heat flickering in his eyes. "So it looks like we're stuck with each other for the entire day."

"Seems so," Matt agreed. He walked toward her, and Jilly's heart sped up. He didn't stop until their bodies were pressed together from chest to knee. And then he destroyed her with one of those toe-curling, exquisite kisses that—

Tasted like chocolate.

Her eyes flew open, and she leaned back to glare at him. "What were you doing while I showered?" she asked, her eyes narrowed on his lips.

"Nothing," he said quickly. Too quickly.

She leaned forward and sniffed. "You smell like chocolate. You *taste* like chocolate. *My* chocolate."

"Aw, now Jilly—"

"Don't you 'Aw, now Jilly' me. There was only *one* piece left. If you ate it, I'm going to sue the pants off you."

"Sweetheart, you don't have to sue me to get my pants off."

"Well, if you ate my last piece of chocolate, you're going to have one hell of a time getting *my* pants off."

He hooked his finger in her towel and pulled. The terry cloth dropped to the floor. "You're not wearing pants." In one smooth movement, he shoved down his boxer briefs and stepped out of them. "And as luck would have it, neither am I."

Her mouth went dry at the sight of him—tall, muscular, aroused, beautiful as only a man with shower-damp, messy hair can be. The desire simmering in his eyes fired an answering want in her.

He drew her into his arms and gently rubbed his erection against her belly, shooting sparks straight to her womb. "I'll have you know," he said, "I only ate *half* of the last chocolate-covered marshmallow. We can buy more when we go out." He bent his head and flicked his tongue over her nipple, stealing her breath.

"I don't know...do you think we'll ever make it out of the room?" she asked, the last word ending with a husky moan as he drew her taut nipple into the heat of his mouth. "I'm afraid that my long abstinence has rendered me a bit insatiable."

"Yeah, that's too bad. Really." He trailed his tongue up her neck then nibbled on her earlobe. "As much as I don't want to leave the room, we're going to have to. We're down to our last condom. *And* the last half of the chocolate-covered marshmallows."

"That candy is mine, Marshmallow-boy."

"Has anyone ever told you that you're really bossy?"

"No one who lived to tell the tale."

"Well, since you shared the last piece of chocolate with me, I'm willing to share my last condom with you. Whaddaya say?"

She pulled his mouth to hers. "I say sharing is good."

SITTING IN THE COMFORTABLE booth where they'd just finished a delicious lunch of seafood pasta, Matt watched Jilly walk toward the sign marked "rest rooms." The instant she disappeared from view, he dragged his hands down his face.

Man, what the hell was wrong with him? Here he was, enjoying the company of a beautiful, intelligent, witty woman who turned him on to the point of forgetting how to speak English and who'd made it plain that another round of heart-stopping sex was in his immediate future. He should be as happy as a pig wallowing in mud. So why wasn't he?

The problem, you doofus, is that you're having too *much fun,* his inner voice informed him.

He huffed out another breath. Damn, it was true. He'd expected to enjoy her *in* bed, but he hadn't anticipated enjoying her just as much *out* of bed. Over lunch they'd discovered a mutual love of Bond flicks, mystery novels, jazz, the zoo, the Metropolitan Museum of Art's latest exhibit, and spicy Thai food. They'd held hands across the table and laughed over high school and college memories. Traded work war stories. Shared favorite Christmas memories.

He wasn't sure how it had happened, but somewhere between the pasta and his second cup of coffee, this weekend with her had entered a very scary place—a danger zone marked by huge, red neon signs that alternately flashed Be Careful, Proceed At Your Own Risk, and Warning: Heartbreak Ahead.

Good God, he really was a doofus. Any other guy would think he'd hit the lottery with this sweet deal he had going—a weekend of mindless, no-strings-attached sex with a woman who could melt bricks. But was he happy? *Noooo.* Well, yes, he was—but not as happy as he should be. Because, unfortunately, Jilly had engaged a hell of a lot more than his body. And he needed to nip that in the bud. Needed some time away from her to put things back in perspective, because any perspective he'd possessed had gotten shot to hell making love to her, and as he'd realized over lunch, that same perspective got shot to hell just talking with her. Yeah. Some time away from her was needed. Just a quick breather. An hour or so would do it.

After pulling out his cell phone, he punched in the number for Chateau Fontaine. One minute later, the proud owner of two spa reservations, he disconnected and blew out a long sigh of relief, assured that he was once again in control.

Seconds later, Jilly reappeared. When she slid into the booth across from him, he said, "I have a confession to make."

Mischief sparkled in her eyes. "Hmmm. Will this one be as good as dropping your old boss's fancy fishing pole overboard when he brought you out on his boat?"

He shot her a mock glare. "I knew I shouldn't have

shared that moment. So I'm not a fisherman. Besides, the pole was slippery, and the water was rough."

"Of course it was," she said, patting his hand, and unsuccessfully hiding her grin. "So what's the big confession?"

"While you were freshening up, I called the resort and arranged for spa time for each of us. At four o'clock I'm scheduled for a massage, and you're in for a deluxe facial."

One brow hiked up. "Facial? You trying to tell me something? Like maybe I'm looking haggard?"

"No way. A guy would have to be insane to tell a woman who's a black belt that she looks haggard. I just thought you might like it."

Something that resembled annoyance flashed in her eyes. She drew a long breath, then said in a cool tone, "Thank you, but I'm perfectly capable of scheduling my own facial, if I decide I want one."

Matt instantly recalled last night's dinner conversation and he mentally slapped his forehead. Jilly would resent any behavior she'd perceive as taking care of her and any man attempting to exert that control. He clasped her hand. She tried to pull away, but he sandwiched her hand between his palms. "I guess I overstepped my bounds by arranging the facial for you, but I meant no offense. I only meant to be polite. I wanted a massage and thought it would be rude to schedule something for myself and leave you out—sort of like opening a box of chocolates and not sharing. Believe it or not, I *do* have some manners." He offered what he hoped was a peacemaking smile. "We can cancel if you'd like, or if you'd rather have a massage, we can change the reservation." He leaned forward. "But I thought *I'd* give you a massage. Later."

The annoyance drained from her gaze. "So, you weren't being bossy and controlling, you were being *nice?*"

"I'm sure you don't mean to sound so shocked. But yeah, *nice* was my intention."

"I see. And I'd be getting a facial *and* a massage."

"That's right."

She leaned forward, and the smoky look in her eyes tightened his groin. "In that case, I'll have the facial. Especially since I probably do look a bit haggard—which, I must point out, is entirely your fault. I didn't get much sleep last night."

"Sweetheart, there is nothing the least bit haggard about you, and you're not going to get much sleep tonight, either."

Their gazes locked, and Matt swore that something passed between them. A warmth, an intimate understanding, that went far beyond the reaches of a casual-sex relationship.

He brought her hand to his mouth and pressed a kiss against her soft palm. "Would you get all mad at me if I offered to pay for lunch?"

"Mad? No. Would I let you? No."

"I like to pay for my dates."

"I'm not your date. I'm your...co-worker. Besides, we're here this weekend on business. This lunch should be charged to our Maxximum corporate account."

I'm not your date. I'm your...co-worker. She was right, of course. Still, an unpleasant sensation hit him at those words. Because, just like dinner last night, this felt very much like a date. And she was more than just his coworker—she was, for the remainder of the weekend, his lover. His inner voice tried to chime in with a reminder that taking Jilly as his lover had been a *baaaaaaad* idea, but as it was too late now, he shoved the irritating voice aside.

"Okay, we'll charge lunch to Maxximum," he agreed. "Ready to do our shopping?"

"Lead on, Marshmallow-condom boy."

"Hey, that's Marshmallow-condom *man* to you."

"You sure you want to argue with a black belt?"

His gaze drifted down to her luscious lips. "Yup. Among other things."

JILLY SAT IN THE SOFT, leather passenger seat of Matt's Lexus, and flipped through the guide to Long Island's wine country. She'd picked up the pamphlet on the way out of the candy shop where she and Matt had each purchased huge boxes of chocolate-covered marshmallows.

"Can't wait to play connect-the-dots with mine," he'd said with a grin that whooshed heat through her.

While Matt drove along Route 25—slowly, due to a heavy volume of cars along the one lane road—Jilly said, "According to this brochure, there are nearly thirty wineries out here." She looked up at him, noting his handsome profile as he watched the road. "That's just amazing. How is it possible that I've lived in New York my entire life and never visited the North Fork?"

"Same for me. The only time I've ever been to this part of Long Island was one summer when my family drove out to Mattituck— I think I was about ten or eleven. One of my dad's bosses had a summer cottage near the beach. I remember we caught clams and steamed them for dinner."

"So I guess you're better at catching clams than you are at catching fish," she teased.

He laughed. "Yeah. Clams don't swim as fast—and you don't need a slippery pole to catch them." He braked for a red light, then looked over at her and smiled. "Would you like to stop at one of the wineries on our way back?"

A perfectly normal smile, and a perfectly simple question. So why did they set her heart to racing? *Because it's Matt's smile. And it's Matt asking the question,* her inner voice sneered.

She ruthlessly pushed the voice aside. Fine. So Matt made her heart go pitty-pat. Next week, she and Kate would find another handsome, intelligent, amusing, sexy man who would affect her in the same way. No problem.

Smiling back, she said, "I'd love to stop at one of the wineries." She forced her gaze back to her brochure. After quickly scanning their choices, she suggested, "How about Galini Vineyards? According to the guide, it's only about a mile up the road. They offer a good selection of wines, and they bottle two different sparkling wines as well. I wouldn't mind picking up a few bottles for myself, and maybe some as Christmas gifts."

"Sounds like a good idea."

They continued the short distance along Route 25. Older houses, set close to the road, their lawns covered with pristine snow, bespoke of Victorian charm with their turrets, porches, and twinkling holiday decorations. A few minutes later, Matt pulled into the gravel driveway marked by a rustic wooden sign entwined with grape leaves proclaiming Galini Vineyards.

"Quaint-looking place," Jilly remarked, peering out the windshield. "It looks more like a farmhouse than a winery."

"You know what they say about looks being deceiving," Matt murmured. "C'mon. Let's check it out."

Hand in hand, they crossed the parking lot, then stomped the snow from their boots, laughing as they tried to see who could stomp the loudest. When they opened the door, bells tingled overhead, and they looked up.

"Hey," Matt said, pointing above the door as he closed it. "That's mistletoe." He waggled his brows. "You know what that means."

Jilly heaved out a put-upon sigh. "I suppose it means I have to kiss you."

"It certainly does."

"Has anyone ever told you that you're a very high-maintenance guy?"

"No one who lived to tell the tale."

Wrapping an arm around her waist, he drew her close, and covered her lips in a warm, friendly, delicious, teasing kiss that kindled a desire for more.

"Ah! I see my mistletoe is working," came a cheerful, Italian-accented voice from behind them.

Arms still around each other, they turned in unison. A robust man whom Jilly judged to be in his mid-fifties smiled at them from an archway leading into another room. He wore faded denim overalls over a cambric shirt, and tan work boots. Gray marked his thick, ebony hair, and his amusement-filled dark eyes regarded them over the rim of a pair of wire-framed reading glasses, which rode the end of his nose.

"Working very well," Matt said with a grin, dropping a quick kiss onto her forehead.

"Every Christmas I hang mistletoe above the door chimes," the man said, walking toward them, wiping his hands on a rag, "and every year I catch dozens of couples kissing. It does my heart good."

Tucking the rag into his pocket, he extended his hand. "Welcome to Galini Vineyards. My name's Joe."

Matt shook the man's hand, then Jilly did the same,

noting Joe's firm handshake and work-roughened, callused hands.

"Are you looking for anything in particular?"

"We understand you have several varieties of sparkling wine?" Jilly said.

"Some very fine varieties," Joe said. He indicated a long, highly polished bar along the left wall. "Would you care for a tasting?"

Jilly smiled. "That would be great."

Joe crossed the room, and Matt and Jilly followed. While Joe readied tulip-shaped glasses and removed bottles from the refrigerator, Jilly looked around the large room.

The rustic theme carried through to the inside of the building. Wood plank floors, paneled walls, and a high, beamed ceiling were made to feel warm and cozy by the stone fireplace nestled in the corner where a fire cheerfully crackled. Attractively framed photographs of the vineyard during various seasons and stages of harvesting lined the walls.

An eye-catching display of wines and handmade ceramic pieces decorated a long table beyond the bar where they now stood. Looking out the huge picture window that took up the entire back wall, Jilly noted that the scenery was identical to that at Chateau Fontaine—row upon row of bare, snow-covered vines, held in place by thick wooden stakes and horizontal cables.

"Incredible to believe that so much of this land where the wineries now are, used to be potato farms," Jilly remarked.

Matt's brows raised. "Potato farms? I didn't know that."

"It's true," Joe said, in his accented voice. "In fact, this very building is a renovated farmhouse. The owners wanted to keep the rustic feel of the place."

"It's terrific," Jilly said, smiling. "Very warm and cozy and friendly."

"*Grazie.* On behalf of the Galini family, I thank you." Joe poured some bubbly into the two glasses. "This is our bestselling sparkling wine. It's crisp, dry, made mostly from pinot noir grapes."

The delicate bubbles burst on Jilly's tongue. "Delicious," she said, and Matt agreed.

They tasted two other sparkling wines, then sampled a merlot and a chardonnay, while Joe related a brief history of the vineyard.

"All the grapes at Galini Vineyards are picked by hand," Joe said, and there was no mistaking the pride in his voice. "We have eighty acres, and grow mostly cabernet sauvignon, chardonnay, merlot, and pinot noir. Five acres are devoted to sangiovese, the grape of—"

"Chianti," Jilly said, with a smile.

Joe beamed at her, his dark eyes filled with pleasure at her knowledge. "Yes. You are a student of wine?"

Jilly laughed. "More like a new recruit. I recently did some research on the subject because a client I'm hoping to win over enjoys wine, and I must admit I find it fascinating." She felt the weight of Matt's gaze and purposely kept her attention focused on Joe. "You must be busy pruning the vines at this time of year."

Joe nodded. "Yes. It is a long, painstaking task. Each individual vine must be pruned manually, and unfortunately not everyone can do it."

"You need to have the feel for it," Jilly guessed.

"That is correct. A full day's work will prune less than half an acre."

"But the hard work is worth it," Matt said. "The wines

are delicious, and this merlot..." he swirled the last swallow in his glass, "is exceptional. And the chardonnay we tasted has a very distinctive oaky flavor."

Joe practically preened from the praise. *"Grazie."*

"That's from aging in oak barrels," Jilly said. "I read all about it. The oak imparts flavor to the wine while it ferments and ages, and because oak is slightly porous, it lets water and alcohol out, and small amounts of oxygen in which helps the wine to 'integrate'..." Her voice trailed off and she laughed at herself. "Sorry. Sometimes I get carried away."

Joe waved his hand. "Nonsense. Your enthusiasm is enchanting."

The bells above the door tinkled as a trio of young men entered. Joe excused himself, and Jilly turned to Matt who regarded her with a look she couldn't decipher.

"You clearly did your homework to prep for this weekend with Jack," he said.

"I'm certain you did the same."

"True, but the Missionary Position Virus problem ate up a lot of my time."

A smile tugged her lips. "Hmmm. Yes, I imagine that the ol' missionary position problem *could* use up a lot of time. Especially if one were to apply themselves to solving that particular problem by coming up with alternate solutions."

"Absolutely," he murmured. He tucked a strand of her hair behind her ear, and her pulse jumped at the intimate gesture. "Have I mentioned that I am an extremely adept problem-solver?"

"No, but you didn't need to. Actions speak louder than words." Sliding her arms around his neck she stood on her toes, leaned into him and lightly bit his earlobe. Feminine satisfaction filled her at the low growl that rumbled in his throat. "So what does *this* action tell you, big guy?" She pressed herself more fully against him.

"That it's time to get out of here."

She leaned back in the circle of his arms and smiled at him. "See? That's one of the things I like about you, Davidson. You're smart."

An undecipherable look flashed in his eyes. "Smart. That's just *one* of the things I like about you, Jilly."

Jilly's heartbeat stuttered. Uh-oh. Once again their lighthearted conversation seemed to veer onto a serious side street. She didn't want him to like her. She didn't want to like him. She just wanted to use him for sex until tomorrow and then forget he existed. Yeah, that's what she wanted.

A frown tugged down her brow. But it was probably okay that he liked her and she liked him. People who engaged in sex *should* like each other—right? Of course! And *like* was a very noncommittal, lukewarm, unintimidating emotion. She *liked* corn on the cob. She *liked* daisies. She *liked* the color green. She *liked* Matt. No big deal. As long as she didn't do something really stupid and *more than like* him, everything would be great.

Stepping back from him, she slipped her hand into his and pulled him toward the table where the colorful handmade ceramic plates, bowls, and cups were displayed.

"What are we doing?" he asked.

"Shopping."

"I'd much rather drag you into that back room and have my wicked way with you behind an oak barrel."

She pushed aside *that* tempting image and shot him a mock frown. "I'm sure that would be very damaging to the wines. Probably disrupt their tannins."

"Whatever they are."

She adopted her most prim, schoolmarm voice. "Tannins are a class of chemicals found in the skins, seeds, and stems of grapes. They're important to wine because they react with oxygen and protect against premature oxidation which is one of the main sources of wine spoilage."

He nuzzled her neck with his warm lips. "Yeah. Premature oxidation. I hate it when that happens."

A giggle erupted from her. "You're distracting me from my shopping." Yet even as she said the words, she turned her head to give him easier access to her neck.

"I can solve this shopping problem in five seconds flat," he said, his breath whispering against her ear. "Let's just buy one of everything and get out of here."

She leaned back in the circle of his arms and shot him a mock frown. "Clearly you know nothing about living on a budget."

"You're right. Let's go get naked and you can tell me all about it."

"And I thought *I* was insatiable."

"Didn't I tell you? Insatiable is my middle name."

"Ha. Since when?"

The amusement drained from his gaze. "Do you really want to know?"

She stilled under the regard of his suddenly serious expression and husky tone. Even as her common sense yelled No!, her lips said, "Yes."

"Ever since I walked into room 312 on Friday night."

His answer stalled her breath, as did the intensity in his gaze. It was what she'd been terrified to hear—yet precisely what she'd wanted him to say. Because she felt exactly the same way.

"You feel it, too," he said softly, his gaze searching hers.

Panic fluttered through her, and her mind screamed at her to lie, to run, to plead the fifth. But what was the point? He'd know she was lying. Besides, she wasn't a liar.

Lifting her chin, she said, "Yes. I feel it, too."

Was that relief that flashed in his eyes? Before she could decide, he cupped her face in his palms and brushed his thumbs over her cheeks. "Question is, what are we going to do about that, Jilly?"

The instant he voiced the question, Matt wished he could snatch back the words. He shouldn't have asked, shouldn't have verbalized the nagging question that had plagued him all day—a certainty reinforced by the wary, guarded look that filled Jilly's eyes and the deafening silence. Man, it was a good thing he'd booked himself that massage because he really did need an hour away from this woman and the potent spell she cast on him.

"We're going to do exactly what we agreed," she finally said. "We're going to enjoy each other the rest of this weekend, then…not enjoy each other anymore. Business as usual."

"You're right, of course." Unfortunately his suspicion that it was going to be impossible for him to hold up his end of their bargain gained momentum with every minute he spent in her company. Especially since it was becoming increasingly obvious that he wouldn't be able to neatly file her away under "Ice Princess" and "enemy number one" any longer.

Forcing what he hoped passed for a carefree grin, he said, "And seeing as how our weekend will be over by this time tomorrow, I vote we head back to the resort and enjoy each other as much as we can for the time we have left." He waggled his brows. "Think we can make it through the entire box of condoms I bought?"

Her expression relaxed and she smiled. "There's only one way to find out. But thirty-six condoms in twenty-four hours?" She shook her head. "I think there'll be a few left over."

"I'm willing to go for the record if you are. Whaddaya say?"

"I say let's finish shopping and get out of here."

Matt selected two platters, both hand painted with grapes, as Christmas gifts for his mom and sister, while Jilly picked out several serving bowls for presents, and two oversize latte cups for herself.

"Latte goes very well with chocolate-covered marshmallows," she said with a teasing grin.

They each picked out several bottles of wine, then brought their purchases to the register where Joe wrapped them in colorful holiday paper while he amused them with stories of growing up in Italy.

While their receipts printed, Joe nodded toward a large glass bowl near the cash register, half-filled with business cards. "We pick a winner once a month for a free bottle of wine. If you'd like to enter, just put your business card in there."

Both Matt and Jilly dug out business cards and passed them to Joe who looked at them with interest. "Maxximum Advertising Agency," he read. "You work together?"

An uncomfortable flush crept up Matt's neck at the unwelcome reminder. "Yes."

Nodding solemnly, Joe dropped the cards into the bowl. "My wife, she works here at the winery. This can sometimes be difficult." He shot them a broad wink. "But sometimes also rewarding." He handed them their packages with a flourish. "Best of luck to you, Matthew and Jillian. I hope you will return to Galini Vineyards. Perhaps in the summer, when the vines are green and lush with ripening fruit. I will give you a personally guided tour."

"That sounds lovely, Joe," Jilly said with a smile. "Thank you."

Matt's stomach tightened. If Jilly meant to take Joe up on his offer, she'd obviously be doing so accompanied by someone who—

Isn't me.

Shoving that disturbing, irritating thought aside, Matt shook Joe's hand, then he and Jilly headed toward the exit. When Matt opened the door, the bells tingled, and they looked up. Once again they stood directly under the mistletoe. Jilly smiled and lifted her face, clearly expecting a quick peck. But need and desire slammed into Matt. Hauling her against him with his free arm, he angled his back to afford them a modicum of privacy, then slanted his mouth over hers in a hot, hard, demanding kiss. When he lifted his head, masculine satisfaction roared through him at Jilly's dazed expression.

"Wow," she breathed. "That's some damn good mistletoe."

Matt looked over his shoulder at Joe, who grinned and shot him a thumbs-up. "Mistletoe works every time," Joe said with a laugh.

With a final wave, they walked to the car. After Matt closed the trunk, he asked, "I'm ready to hit the room, get naked, and start working on that thirty-six pack. Whaddaya say?"

"I say it's good to set high goals in life."

9

RELAXED, REJUVENATED, and all but purring from her deluxe facial, Jilly walked toward the resort's bar where she and Matt had agreed to meet for an after-spa drink before returning to the room to ready themselves for dinner with Jack.

She sat in an overstuffed chair at a small, round table that afforded her a good view of the lobby area so she wouldn't miss Matt. She checked her watch. Good. She had at least ten or fifteen minutes before Matt showed up. After slipping her cell phone from her purse, she quickly dialed Kate's number. Her friend picked up on the second ring.

"I've been dying to hear from you," Kate said. "How's it going?"

Jilly blew out a breath. "Remember how you suggested that maybe I should indulge in an affair with Matt this weekend? That it would satisfy my curiosity so then I'd be able to forget him? And that as long as we both went into it understanding it would be over after this weekend, everything would be fine?"

"Yes, yes, and yes. I remember perfectly. So? How are things?"

"Good and bad."

"Good first."

"You can't call me Rusty anymore."

"Ooohhh. So what *can* I call you?"

"How about Lucky?"

"How lucky?"

"Hit-the-jackpot lucky."

Kate gave a low whistle. "So what's the bad part?"

"The plan to satisfy my curiosity so then I'd be able to forget him isn't working out all that well. My curiosity is far from satisfied, and I think it's going to prove a lot more difficult than I'd thought to drop this man off my radar screen after tomorrow."

"I see. So you like him."

Jilly pinched the bridge of her nose. "I'm afraid so."

"Well, you know, there's no law that says you can't continue this once you return to work."

"Yes, there is. Engaging in an affair at work is professional suicide. Especially since whoever wins the ARC account is going to be the other one's *boss*. I get queasy just thinking about *that* scenario. Besides, there's more to it than just that. Matt just isn't my type."

"Oh. So you only like him when you're both naked?"

Jilly frowned. If only that were true. "Not exactly."

"Well, what's wrong with him?"

Frustration edged through Jilly—at Matt for causing her all this turmoil, and at herself for allowing him to. "He's just...a very take-charge guy. You know how I don't like that."

"So he's stepping on your independence."

"Exactly!"

"How?"

"He's...crowding me. Like today, we went out and he offered to pay for my lunch. And then he scheduled a deluxe facial at the spa's resort for me. And then he bought me a bottle of wine. I am perfectly capable of purchasing my own meal, my own wine, and arranging my own facials."

"Of course you are. That bastard. Does his cruelty never end? You want me to drive out there and kick his smarmy ass?"

Jilly squeezed her eyes shut. "Ha, ha. Point taken. But it's small stuff like that which shows the sort of person he is."

"Thoughtful and romantic?"

"If you'll recall, things with Aaron started out nicely as well. Then the next thing I knew, he expected me to re-arrange my life to revolve around his."

"Yes, but if *you'll* recall, Aaron also eventually proved not to have a thoughtful or romantic bone in his body."

"Hey, whose side are you on?"

"Yours, silly. But I'd hate to see you throw away something that might turn out to be just what you're looking for."

"But I'm not looking for anything!"

"*Everyone* is looking for something, Jilly. I clearly remember you saying you'd snap up the right guy if he came along."

"Well, Matt is *not* the right guy."

"You know what I think your problem is?" Kate asked in a serious voice.

"I'm almost afraid to ask."

"You should be, because I don't think you're going to like the answer. Shall I continue anyway?"

"Might as well," Jilly groused. "What else are best friends for but to make you feel miserable?"

"I think that you're confused and out of sorts because you really like his man and you didn't expect to. You suspect you could easily *more than like* him, and that scares you—for all the reasons caring for someone scares any-body, but also because a relationship with Matt could negatively impact your career. And you, more than anyone I know, define yourself by your career."

"Okay, what are you—psychic?"

"No. I'm in love. I know the signs."

Panic fluttered in Jilly's stomach. "Good grief, don't even *whisper* the 'L' word. That would be a complete disaster."

"Listen, that's what I thought about Ben. And when I realized I was falling in love with him, I was scared to death. But I took a chance, put my heart on the line, and look how great things turned out."

"I am *not* falling in love with Matt."

"If you say so."

"I say so. I'm just annoyed at myself for liking him." *Liking him waaaaay too much.* "And annoyed at him for being so...likable. Damn it, I don't want to like him. I want to *forget* him."

"Well, the only way to forget about a man is to find another man."

"Excellent. I'm making that job one as soon as I get home. You'll help me, right?"

"Of course. Maybe you should even look around at the resort. Might be someone right under your nose."

"Maybe I will."

"I do have to warn you, Jilly—there's one hitch to the plan of forgetting a man by finding another man."

"What's that?"

"It only works if you aren't in love with the guy you're trying to forget."

"Then we shouldn't have any problem, because I am so *not* in love with Matt."

"Good."

"Fine."

"So are you going to sleep with him tonight?"

"Of course. I'm not in love with him, but I'm seriously in *lust* with him. In fact, I'd better go. I'm expecting him soon."

"All right. Enjoy the rest of your weekend, and call me when you get home tomorrow. We'll plan to hit a few clubs after work on Tuesday so the forgetting can officially begin."

"Sounds terrific. Bye." Jilly disconnected and slipped her phone into her purse.

Sounds terrific? She blew out a long sigh. If only. Unfortunately, going clubbing to forget about Matt sounded the exact *opposite* of terrific.

MATT WALKED TOWARD THE BAR feeling like a new man. Yup, an hour-long massage had worked out all his kinks and tensions and put everything back into perspective. All he'd needed was an hour to himself, away from that distracting woman, to get his head back on straight.

The remainder of the weekend was clearly mapped out in his mind. Meet Jilly, have drink, go back to room, enjoy a quickie, get dressed, have dinner with Jack where he'd make subtle inroads in his quest to win the ARC account, go back to the room with Jilly, enjoy another bout—or two, possibly three—of sex, sleep, have one more possible bout of morning sex, pack and get out of Dodge. Then business as usual. Perfect. His plan was like a well-oiled machine.

Unfortunately his well-oiled machine suffered a cog in its wheel as he rounded the corner and the bar came into view. His gaze instantly zeroed in on Jilly. Jilly, dressed in a pale blue turtleneck and loose-fitting, casual athletic pants, sitting alone at small, round table. Jilly, with her dark, shiny hair curling around her shoulders. Jilly, smiling and laughing—with the guy sitting alone at the table next to hers. A guy who, Matt noted grimly, was looking at Jilly as if she were an ice-cream cone from which he wanted to take a big, long lick.

There was no mistaking the unpleasant sensation that hit him like a punch in the heart. Jealousy, pure and simple. And not simply because the guy was showing interest in Jilly—while Matt didn't like it, he couldn't blame him. No, it was more the fact that Jilly was smiling and laughing with the jerk instead of using one of her black belt moves to toss him onto his flirtatious ass.

She's not yours, man, his inner voice chimed in.

Like hell. Maybe she wasn't his for the long run, but she *was* his for the remainder of this weekend. And he wasn't about to share her with that damn Brad Pitt lookalike.

Drawing a deep, calming breath, he walked toward the bar. As he neared their tables, the Pitt lookalike rose and passed her a business card. "I'd love to stay and talk, but I'm meeting an associate at a restaurant in town," Matt overheard him say with regret in his voice. "My office is just a few blocks from yours. Call me if you'd like to get together."

Pitt-boy moved off. Bludgeoning back his jealousy, Matt unclenched his jaw and walked the last few feet to the table, then sat down across from Jilly.

She greeted him with a smile. "Hi."

"Hi." He jerked his head toward the retreating man. "Who's that?" Damn it, he hadn't meant to ask the second he sat down. But at least he'd managed to keep his voice casual.

She gave a nonchalant shrug and, much to his annoyance, slipped the guy's business card into her purse. "Just a guy who was sitting at the next table. His name is

Brad and he's a dentist. His office is close to Maxximum's."

Matt resisted the urge to look heavenward. Figures the guy's name really was Brad. Or maybe he'd changed his name from something really nerdy *to* Brad to match his looks.

"A dentist, huh? Well, that explains it."

"Explains what?"

"Why he eyeballed you like he wanted to clean your teeth—with his tongue."

She blinked in obvious surprise, then raised her eyebrows. "Did it ever occur to you that *if* he looked at me that way it might be because he found me attractive—not because he was a dentist?"

Damn it, he felt like an ass. A disgruntled ass. A jealous, disgruntled ass. He should have kept his mouth shut. "I didn't mean to imply otherwise. It was very obvious that he found you attractive." Giving himself a severe mental shake, he forced a smile. "Can't fault the guy on his taste."

"Thank you." For several seconds her gaze searched his. "For a minute there you sounded like a jealous lover."

It was impossible to tell from her tone if that idea annoyed or pleased her. Opting for the unvarnished truth, he said, "I *am* a jealous lover—right now. Starting Tuesday, I won't be, but for the short remainder of this three-day weekend, you're mine." He shot her a questioning look. "Unless you've had a change of heart?"

"No," she said quickly.

A breath he hadn't even realized he held eased from him, and he refused to examine the depth of his relief.

"So, how was your massage?" she asked.

I need another one, thanks to Brad the dentist. "It was great. How about the facial?"

She closed her eyes and gave an exaggerated shiver. "Incredible. I feel like a new woman."

"Yeah? Hard to believe you could feel any better than you already did." Reaching out, he grasped her hand, and brought it to his lips. He pressed a kiss to her palm, liking the way her eyes darkened at the gesture. "I vote we skip the drinks and go upstairs so you can show me all that gorgeous, pampered skin."

Her gaze skimmed over him in a way that hiked his blood pressure into the danger zone. "Hmmm. Will you show me all your pampered, relaxed muscles in return?"

"You show me yours, I'll show you mine. Whaddaya say?"

"I say showing is good."

They made their way, hand in hand, to the elevator. Impatience pulled at him, and his hands all but itched to touch her. He couldn't recall ever wanting to touch a woman this badly. Apparently she was suffering from the same impatience because the instant the elevator doors closed, surrounding them in privacy, she pressed him against the wall, and pulled his head down to hers.

He kissed her with all the raw, edgy, pent-up need pounding through him, need sharpened all the more by her urgency.

She rubbed herself against his erection, then leaned back to look at him with a devilish, smoky-eyed expression. "Uh-oh. I don't think your massage worked. You're obviously not nearly as relaxed as you should be."

"All your fault, I'm afraid."

"Then you must allow me to fix it."

"Consider me at your disposal."

She wound her arms around his neck, and arched

against him, her tongue dancing with his. His hands skimmed under the thin cotton of her shirt to touch her warm, soft skin. A low, pleasure-filled moan vibrated in her throat, and he kissed his way down her neck to touch his tongue to the sound.

The elevator stopped and the doors slid open. They circled down the hallway, kissing, hands searching. He slipped the key card from his back pocket and managed to open the door, not an easy task with Jilly's distracting hands sliding under his shirt.

Heart knocking against his ribs, he pushed the door closed behind them with his foot. As she had in the elevator, she urged his back against the wall. Breaking off their frantic kiss, she grabbed the ends of his Polo shirt, and he raised his arms so she could pull it over his head. The striped cotton fell to the floor. When he reached for her, she grabbed his wrists and gently pressed them against the wall.

Their gazes locked and he groaned. With her lips wet and reddened from their kiss, her eyes glittering with desire, her hair messed from his hands, she looked aroused, tempting and sinful.

"Let me touch you," she whispered.

He had to swallow to find his voice. "I'm all yours, sweetheart."

A sexy half smile curved her lips, and in a heartbeat she switched tempo on him, shifting from fast forward to slow seduction. She nipped soft kisses along his jaw and neck while her fingertips glided up and down his torso. His eyes slid shut, and he had to press his fists against the wall to keep them from reaching for her.

She kissed her way across his chest, dragging her tongue across his nipples, then drawing them into the warmth of her mouth, all while her fingers played gently over his abdomen. She licked and kissed her way lower, her mouth leaving a trail of damp heat. When her fingers brushed beneath the waistband of his jeans, his muscles jerked and a low groan pushed past his lips. Her silky hair brushed over his stomach as she sunk to her knees and unfastened his jeans.

Opening his eyes, he looked down and watched her free his erection then slowly draw him into her mouth. He hissed in a sharp breath, and slipped his fingers into her hair, absorbing the erotic, arousing sight of her lips gliding over him, the incredible feel of her tongue slowly circling him, the sensation of her hands cupping him, her fingertips brushing over his sensitive skin.

She drew him deeper into her mouth, dragging a growl from his throat. His entire body tightened with the need to come, and he knew he wouldn't be able to hold off his orgasm much longer.

Grasping her upper arms, he urged her upward. "Can't take anymore," he whispered against her mouth, as he toed off his loafers. "Want you. Need you. *Now.*"

Without a word, she stepped back and yanked her turtleneck over her head and unfastened her bra. While he shoved down his jeans and boxers and stepped out of them, she kicked off her flat shoes then skimmed her drawstring cotton pants and lace panties down her hips. Naked, she entwined their fingers, then led him to the bed.

"Lie down," she whispered. She quickly grabbed a condom from their new supply. Straddling his thighs, she tore the packet, rolled the latex over his erection, then slowly sank herself onto him.

He gritted his teeth against the sweet torture of her leisurely movements as she lifted herself until he almost left her body, then slowly glided down, burying him deep in her snug, velvety heat once again.

He palmed her full breasts, his fingers grazing her taut nipples, his senses exploding from the sight of her astride him, the feel of her inner walls surrounding him, squeezing him, the scent of their mutual arousal rising between them. His gaze riveted on the sight of his erection sliding into her body, and his fight for control was irrevocably lost.

Grasping her hips, he reared up to a sitting position, and drew one of her erect nipples into his mouth. Her nails dug into his shoulders, she arched her back, a long moan rumbling in her throat. He felt her tighten around him, grind against him, and his orgasm ripped through him. Burying his face between her breasts, he held on tight and whispered her name like a prayer while the tremors shook him.

When his breathing returned to normal, he lifted his head. Her head hung down loosely, like a rag doll left in the rain, shiny skeins of tangled dark hair obscuring her face. Touching his fingers to her jaw, he urged her chin up. Their eyes met, and the area surrounding his heart went hollow, only to then fill with a sensation unlike anything he'd ever before experienced.

He released her hips, then traced his fingers over her face with hands that were noticeably unsteady, like a blind man seeing her features through touch. He felt the strong need to say something, but a lump of emotion he couldn't, didn't even want to, try to explain clogged his throat. Leaning forward, he rested his forehead against hers and murmured the only word he could manage— the one that seemed to sum up all he was feeling.

"Jilly."

Her fingers skimmed through his hair, and her warm

breath brushed past his lips. She said only word in reply, but it was enough.

"Matt."

AN HOUR LATER, JILLY GAVE herself one last quick check in the full-length mirror before they left the room to join Jack for dinner. Dressed in a tailored, white, French-cuffed shirt tucked into her favorite black, slim skirt that skimmed her knees, and strappy Ralph Lauren heels, she looked calm, cool, and professional. From the neck down.

From the neck up, she looked like a woman who had just been thoroughly and magnificently loved. Even her prim chignon could not disguise the glow in her eyes, the rosy flush of her complexion, the slight swelling of her lips. She might as well have pasted a sign on her forehead that read, *Yes, I just did it—twice, in fact. And I can't wait to do it again.*

Matt stepped behind her, and their gazes met in the mirror. Heat whooshed through her at the barely banked fire in his serious, dark-blue gaze. Sliding his hands around her waist, he drew her back against him, then bent his head and nuzzled her neck with his warm lips. She really needed to step away from him. Instead she arched her neck to give him better access.

"You look beautiful, Jilly," he murmured against her ear, sending heated shivers down her spine. His hands skimmed upward, cupping her breasts through her shirt, stalling her breath. "And you smell incredible. What is that scent you wear?"

Okay, she'd tell him as soon as she remembered how to speak. Drawing a deep breath, she said, "It's called Clean Laundry."

He lifted his head and looked at her reflection in the mirror, his surprise evident. "You're kidding."

"Nope." No need to tell him that his distracting touch had rendered her incapable of doing anything as complicated as "kidding."

"That's exactly what you smell like. Clean laundry that's been hanging outdoors in the sunshine."

She managed a smile at his reflection, trying not to concentrate on the sight and feel of his hands cupping her breasts. "Thus the name of the cologne. The same perfume company makes several interesting scents I like. Another favorite is Angel Food Cake."

"Sounds delicious." His teeth gently closed over her earlobe. "Good enough to eat."

She briefly squeezed her eyes shut, allowing herself to wallow in the pleasure the images *that* evoked, before she turned to face him.

"Listen," she said, trying but spectacularly failing to ignore his erection pressing against her and his hands running slowly down her back, "if you don't stop touching me and looking at me like that, we'll never make it to dinner. And even if we do, Jack will know exactly how we've been spending our time."

"Since he met that woman, it's pretty clear he's spending his time exactly the same way."

"And that's fine. But this dinner is *business*. Let's keep it that way." Grasping his hands, she forcibly planted them against his sides, then wagged her finger at him. "No touching until we're back in the room."

He blew out a long sigh. "I guess that means no kissing, either."

"That's right."

"Fondling?"

"Out of the question."

He shot her a mock frown. "Is *looking* at you okay?"

"Sure. As long as you don't look at me in *that way*."

"What way?"

"In that 'I'd like to spread you between two slices of bread and gobble you up' way."

"Hmmm...yeah. That's exactly what I want for dinner." He leaned back against the wall, shot her a half smile and a wink. "Any chance you're on the menu?"

Oh, boy. This was bad. She was a total sucker for a sexy guy winking at her. It was irrational, ridiculous, idiotic, and inexplicable—but there it was. That wink turned her insides to mush. They needed to get out of the room. Now. Before she gave into temptation and removed his pale blue cashmere pullover and navy dress pants and reminded herself of just how good *he* tasted.

After snatching up her purse, she headed toward the door. "I'm on the dessert menu. But you have to be a good boy. Remember—no dessert until dinner is finished."

The ride in the elevator was a torturous exercise in restraint. They stood on opposite ends, staring at each other in silence. Finally Matt cleared his throat. "I just want you to know that even though I want you naked, I realize this is a business dinner and will behave myself accordingly."

"Excellent. And even though I want *you* naked, I realize this is a business dinner and will behave myself accordingly."

He erased the distance between them with two long strides, bracketing his arms on either side of her. Only inches separated them, and although he didn't actually touch her, the warmth emanating from his body heated her as if he'd lit a fire under her skirt. "But after dinner, all bets are off, Jilly." The low words whispered close to her ear, sending desire shuddering through her.

Damn him. No fair. Why hadn't he stayed on his side of the elevator? Now she was all flushed. And distracted. Clearly he'd shifted into his take-charge mode to have the last word. Typical.

The elevator stopped and he stepped away from her. They crossed the lobby in silence, their shoes tapping against the polished marble. As the maître d' led them toward the table, she looked at Matt over her shoulder.

"Matt?"

"Yes?"

"I'm not wearing any underwear."

10

MATT HALTED AS IF HE'D WALKED into a brick wall and stared at Jilly following the maître d', her words reverberating through his mind. *I'm not wearing any underwear.*

His gaze zeroed in on her shapely butt. Heat sizzled through him, and he ran his hands down his face. Wrapped in that black skirt that offered nothing more overt than a hint at her curves, she looked as good from the back as she did from the front.

Forcing his feet to move forward, he inwardly chuckled—at himself. He'd thought he'd cleverly gotten in the last word. Well, she'd shut him up but good. He only hoped that when he did finally locate his voice, the first thing that flopped out of his mouth wouldn't be *Jilly isn't wearing any underwear.*

Bludgeoning back thoughts of *that*, and shifting his gaze away from her butt, he quickened his pace to catch up, and focused his attention on the table set in the far corner where Jack sat opposite a blond woman. Must be the lady friend Jack had met. A fissure of annoyance edged through him that Jack had included her in their business dinner, but there wasn't much he could do about it. Besides, maybe it was for the best. The more people, the more conversation, the more to concentrate on besides Jilly—who wasn't wearing any underwear. Another bolt of heat shot through him. Damn. She'd picked a hell of a night to go commando.

When they arrived at the table, Jack rose to greet them, then introduced his new friend, Carol Webber. Matt shook hands with the attractive blonde, whom he placed in her early thirties. Once Jilly and Matt were seated opposite each other, Jack asked, "So what did you two do today?"

"Some holiday shopping, and we visited another winery," Jilly said with a smile as she settled her napkin on her lap.

"And managed not to kill each other?" Jack asked with a laugh. "That's quite a feat for competing co-workers."

"We came close a couple of times," Jilly said, "but my facial and Matt's massage this afternoon took the edge off."

"Isn't the facial marvelous?" Carol asked. "I had one yesterday, and I *still* feel all tingly."

"Oh, I'm definitely still tingly," Jilly agreed.

She was looking at Carol, her voice was perfectly neutral, but Matt knew the words were directed at him. And damn it, he was more than tingly. He was hard. And uncomfortable. And annoyed. It was freakin' difficult to think of something intelligent to say to the man whose account you hoped to win when all Matt could do was hope he wouldn't have to stand up for any reason. He hadn't experienced a problem like this since high school. When the hell had his penis spawned into this out of control appendage?

Friday night, his inner voice informed him, *around 3:00 a.m. When you entered 312 and found the current Miss Commando wearing that damn black satin getup.*

Matt wrestled back the image of a sexy, disheveled Jilly from his mind, shifted to relieve the strangulation occurring in the front of his slacks, then asked Jack, "How did your day trip to Orient Point go?"

Jack embarked on a lengthy retelling of his day, with numerous flirty interruptions from Carol, and Matt heaved an inward sigh of relief that the conversational ball was out of his court, temporarily requiring nothing more from him than a nod, and a few noncommittal phrases. The talk turned to food, and they chatted, perused the menu, and Matt began to relax.

After the waiter took their orders, Matt turned to Carol. "What sort of work do you do?" he asked.

"I'm a nurse. Jack tells me you and Jilly work in advertising, and that you're both vying for his company's account." Her gaze bounced between him and Jilly. "That must be making for an interesting weekend."

"It certainly hasn't been dull," Matt agreed.

"You're both very creative," Carol said with a smile. "Jack told me all about your presentations, and they're both wonderful. I can't imagine how he'll be able to choose."

Matt glanced at Jilly, and he stilled when their gazes met. Something unspoken seemed to pass between them, something that Matt couldn't put his finger on, but he knew it boded very poorly for his competitive instincts. He should have grabbed Carol's comment and sprinted toward the end zone with it, subtly stating reasons why Jack should choose his presentation over Jilly's. But he remained mute, unable to utter a word.

"Well, speaking of choosing," Jack said, striding into the awkward silence, "I need to choose whether I want to take the mud bath or the seaweed wrap tomorrow morning before heading back to the city. Anybody have any ideas on that?"

The conversation veered onto nonwork-related topics, and Matt made a concentrated effort to participate. And he was doing a damn good job of it, too, until midway through his entrée, when something nudged his shin under the table. As the table was quite small, he moved his leg slightly to get it out of the way, while continuing to listen to Carol's story about a Caribbean cruise she'd taken last year. But seconds later, he was nudged again. And then he felt the unmistakable glide of a shoeless foot slipping up his pant leg.

He froze, his forkful of chicken arrested halfway to his mouth. His gaze swiveled to Jilly who resembled the picture of innocence—except for the telltale crimson stain rising on her cheeks—a stain that surely wasn't caused by Carol's retelling of her shopping adventures in the Caribbean straw market.

He tried to move his leg away, but there wasn't much room to maneuver, and she was persistent, brushing her foot over his shin.

A combination of irritation and desire nipped at him at her tactics. Clearly she'd abandoned their agreement to stick to business during dinner, and while he couldn't deny he liked her attentions, he didn't care for her timing.

Shooting her a warning glare, which she missed as her attention remained focused on Carol, he moved his leg again. And again her toes followed, gliding over his pants, this time inching higher, past his knee, and onto his thigh.

Damn it, enough was enough. Two could play at this game. If she thought—

She pushed back her chair and rose. Sizzling him with a pointed look that appeared to throw more daggers than Cupid's arrows, she murmured, "Please excuse me. I need to visit the ladies' room."

Matt mentally counted to ten, then rose. "Excuse me, please. Men's room." He walked swiftly toward the archway through which Jilly had disappeared. After turning two corners, he reached the rest rooms. She stood outside the ladies' room, hands on hips, shoe tapping against the marble floor, her narrowed eyeballs all but emitting steam.

"What the hell are you doing?" she said, her voice an angry hiss.

He simply stared. *"Me?"*

"Yes, you. When we agreed that this dinner was strictly business, that didn't mean *monkey* business."

"Something you might want to recall, Miss I'm Not Wearing Underwear."

"I only said that because you pulled your macho take-charge act in the elevator."

His gaze skimmed over her skirt. "So does that mean you're really wearing underwear?"

Her eyes narrowed further, and she crossed her arms over her chest. "That's not the point right now—"

"No, it's not," he agreed, stepping closer to her. "The point is that for someone who claims she prides herself on playing fair, you've been cheating. I'll play by whatever set of guidelines you want, but the next time you decide to switch rules, I'd appreciate it if you'd deal me in."

"You're a fine one to talk," she said, her eyes glittering with obvious anger. "What, are you pissed because I wouldn't participate in your little game of footsie?"

"You call that not participating? For God's sake, your foot was practically in my crotch." A frown tugged down his brows. "And what do you mean *my* little game of footsie?"

"What do *you* mean my foot was practically in your crotch? I didn't touch you."

"Well, I didn't touch you, either."

Her eyes widened. "Wait a minute. Are you telling me that wasn't your foot caressing me under the table?"

"Yes. Are you telling me that wasn't your foot snaking up my leg?"

She held her hand over her heart. "Swear." They stared at each other in silence for several seconds, then she said, "It was definitely a man's foot making nice-nice with me. So if it wasn't you, it had to be Jack."

"And the foot making familiar with me was definitely a woman's—so it must have been Carol." He cleared his throat. "Sorry for thinking you'd played foul."

"Apology accepted—and extended back. Sorry." Jilly blew out a breath. "I guess the only question remaining is did they mean to fondle *us?* Or were they trying to fondle each other and we just got in the way?"

Matt's jaw tightened. "That bastard. He damn well better not have been making a pass at you."

"I agree. I knew Jack wouldn't win any Mr. Charming prizes, but what a lousy thing to do, with his date sitting right there."

"Yeah," Matt agreed, although that wasn't at all what he'd meant. Anger pumped through him that Jack had dared to touch her, an emotion that wasn't calmed at all by the recollection that she might not be wearing panties. "Just how friendly did he manage to get with you?"

"I stood up when he reached my knee." She blew out a breath. "This is no less awkward for you. After all, the date of the man you're trying to impress might be making the moves on you."

"Definitely awkward," Matt agreed.

"Surely they thought they were touching each other."

"I don't know. While I was talking to Carol, I noticed Jack sort of giving you the eye." *The bastard.*

"Unfortunately I think you might be right. He made a few comments that definitely skidded the line."

"Oh? And how did you respond?"

Her expression cooled to a mask of chilled detachment. "The same way I've responded every time I've been placed in a similar situation. With professional courtesy and nothing more. I told you—I don't play footsie, or any other games, with clients." Lifting her chin, she asked, "So, how do we handle this potential problem?"

"Personally, I think it's time for the meal to end. If they were trying to make the moves on each other, it's time for them to be alone. And if either of them was making a move on either one of us, it's *way* past time for this meal to end."

"All right. But let's try not to make it a totally obvious getaway. How about I plead a headache and leave, and then you can make your escape about ten minutes later?"

"Fine."

She made to move past him, clearly intent upon returning to the table. Extending a hand, he snagged her arm. She looked at him with that same cool detachment, an expression that filled him with an uncomfortable sense of loss he didn't like one bit.

When he remained silent, she raised her brows. "Did you want something, Matt?"

Yes. I want you to stop looking at me with that dismissive expression, and look at me with that smoky, aroused look I love. Drawing a deep breath, he said, "Yes. I want you to know that I realize you don't play those sort of games with clients, and if you thought I implied otherwise, I'm sorry." He took a step closer to her, inhaling her clean scent, the backs of his fingers brushing against the warm, outer curve of her breast. With his gaze steady on hers, he said, "And I want you to know that if Carol *was* putting a move on me, I'm definitely not interested."

"Not that it's any of my business, but I think you'd be insane to risk it, what with Jack sitting right there."

"Jack has nothing to do with my disinterest in Carol."

Something indecipherable flashed in her eyes. Good. At least she didn't look quite so impassive anymore. "Anything else?" she asked.

"Yeah. When you return to the room, don't get undressed. I want to discover for myself what you are, or aren't, wearing under that skirt."

BUMPING THE DOOR TO ROOM 312 closed with her hip, Jilly tossed her clutch purse onto the dresser and paced to the window. She only had a few minutes before Matt arrived, and she badly needed a precoital pep talk.

Okay, it didn't matter that Carol had most likely known damn well whose leg she was exploring. And it wouldn't have mattered if Matt had taken the blonde up on her offer. He was attractive and single, and after tomorrow, no concern of Jilly's.

Of course, that didn't explain her profound relief that Matt hadn't found Carol attractive, or the unpleasant sting of jealousy that another woman had touched him.

"Argh," she moaned. "Listen, you ding-a-ling," she muttered to herself. "Suck it up and deal with reality. After tomorrow, he's not yours." An ache she couldn't name invaded the area surrounding her heart, and her breath caught.

"All right," she whispered. "But tonight he *is* mine. And I'm going to make the most of it."

No sooner had the words passed her lips, than the phone rang. Grabbing up the receiver, she said, "Hello?"

"Miss Taylor?" asked a perky, feminine voice.

"Yes."

"This is Maggie at the front desk. We have a delivery for you. Could you please come down to the lobby to sign for it?"

"Delivery? What is it?"

"I couldn't say. It's in a box."

"Can someone bring it up?"

"I'm sorry, Miss Taylor, but deliveries must be signed for by the recipient in the lobby. It's required by the resort's security policy."

"I understand. I'll be right down." Probably some work-related papers from Adam. She scribbled a quick note to Matt, then exited the room. When she arrived at the front desk several minutes later, Maggie greeted her with a smile.

"Your package is in the back room, Miss Taylor. I'll be just a moment."

Jilly waited, and waited, and waited, barely resisting the urge to climb over the counter and storm the Employees Only door through which Maggie had disappeared nearly ten minutes earlier and shout, *A very sexy man is waiting for me. Could we please hurry this up a bit?*

Snatching up the house phone, she dialed room 312, but Matt didn't answer. Curious. He should have been in the room by now. Her gaze drifted toward the restaurant. Was Matt still in there with Jack and Carol? If so, it was taking him a while to escape. She stilled as a nasty suspicion curled through her. Maybe he wasn't trying to escape at all. Maybe he was in there making the most of his solo time by selling Jack on his ideas for ARC.

"Here you are, Miss Taylor." Maggie's breathless voice yanked her attention back. "I'm so sorry for the delay."

Jilly stared at the long, gold rectangular box Maggie held out to her. "What is this?"

"Your delivery," Maggie said with a laugh.

"It looks like a florist's box," Jilly murmured, taking the package, and admiring the intricate red and green bow.

"It does," Maggie agreed, with an unmistakable envious sigh. "It seems you have an admirer."

Jilly tried to ignore the quickening of her heart, and failed completely. After scribbling her name on the ledger Maggie slid across the desk, Jilly moved to the end of the counter and slowly lifted the lid.

Two dozen pure white roses lay nestled in a bed of red tissue paper. A single sprig of bright green mistletoe sprang from the center of the bouquet. The heady floral scent wafted up to her, and she breathed deeply, her eyes closing with pleasure. She couldn't recall the last time a man had sent her flowers. Her senior prom, maybe?

A small, white envelope rested in a fold of the tissue paper, and she slid it out with hands that weren't quite steady. Pulling out the card, she read: *I bought white roses as a memento of things that remind me of you—snowballs and marshmallows. Let's make the most of our last night together. I thought the mistletoe might come in handy. I'm waiting...*

Jilly's insides turned to mush, and she heaved out a gushy, feminine sigh. A slap of shame immediately followed on the heels of that sigh for thinking Matt was still in the restaurant schmoozing Jack when he'd been buying her flowers—a sweet, thoughtful, romantic gesture that touched her in ways she didn't dare examine too closely. Because they scared her. And because, as he'd written himself, this was their last night together.

After tucking the note back into the tissue paper, she

closed the lid, then carried the box toward the elevator. It was time to make the most of their last night together.

As she approached room 312, she drew a deep breath in a futile effort to calm her jittery insides. More than mere anticipation jangled her nerves. Where had this sudden nervousness come from? Her irritating inner voice coughed to life. *It comes from the fact that more than just great sex awaits you in room 312. That man and his roses have heartbreak written all over them.*

Her gaze drifted over the floral box she cradled. She suspected her inner voice was right on target, giving Jilly the sudden sinking sensation that she stood with a big bull's-eye painted on her heart—right in front of an ammo-laden Matt.

Self-directed annoyance straightened her spine and lifted her chin. She simply wouldn't allow her heart to turn this weekend into more than it was—a fun, no-strings romp. So what if Matt had turned out to be much more than she'd expected? Her expectations of him had been so low, anything he said or did of a nonheinous nature would appear disproportionately good. Next week she and Kate would find her a man who wasn't her co-worker or rival. And who didn't possess the take-charge chromosome. Yes indeed, they'd find her a better man. A sexier man. Okay, *that* would present a challenge. But, hey, she thrived on challenges. Challenges were good. Challenges built character. She loved challenges. Yup, she sure did.

Drawing a final, bracing breath, she slid her key card into the door and entered. And halted.

Matt leaned against the desk, his ankles casually crossed, but there was nothing casual about the desire burning in his gaze. Her heart stuttered at that heated look. Forcing her feet to move, she walked slowly toward him, desperately searching for some levity in a situation that didn't feel at all like a lighthearted romp. It felt intense, leaving her weak-kneed and vulnerable in a way she hadn't anticipated, and didn't like.

She swallowed to find her voice, then forced a smile. "Someone sent me flowers," she said lightly. "The card wasn't signed. I think maybe they're from the guy in 311—"

She halted as the bed came into view. White rose petals were scattered over the forest-green bedspread. The night table had been cleared, and now held a large silver platter filled with grapes, strawberries, and two dome-covered plates. Two champagne glasses sat next to the platter, as well as a silver ice bucket with the slender neck of a dark green bottle peeking over the rim.

Before she could locate her missing voice, he walked toward her and said, "The flowers are from the guy in 312."

Yanking her gaze from the bed and tray, she asked, "What's all this?"

"Dessert. Since we didn't have it in the restaurant, I ordered it to go. Thought you might enjoy a picnic—in bed."

Surely there must have been, at some point over the course of her life, an event that she'd enjoyed more than the prospect of a picnic in bed with Matt, but darned if she could think of what that event might have been.

When he halted in front of her, she said, "You went to a lot of trouble."

"I don't consider it 'trouble' to make our last night together memorable."

"I think it would have been memorable even without all this."

"True." His lips curved upward, but his smile looked

tight and didn't quite reach his eyes. "But I like to be a tough act to follow."

No problem there. In fact, she very much feared Matt would prove an *impossible* act to follow. "I see." She nodded toward the dessert tray. "How do you know I'll like what you ordered?"

"I know what you like, Jilly," he said in a low, deep voice that shimmied heated awareness down her spine. "Would you like me to prove it?"

Probably she nodded. She certainly meant to, but the anticipation brought on by his question, and the desire emanating from him, rendered her immobile. Clearly she gave him some sort of affirmative gesture because he gently took the floral box from her, and set it on a chair. Then he wrapped one strong arm around her waist, tunneled his other hand into her chignon and, before she could utter a sound, kissed her with an unrestrained passion that liquefied her knees. Hot, hungry and demanding, his mouth slanted over hers, his tongue rubbing against hers with a delicious friction that pooled desire low in her belly.

Jilly circled her arms around his neck and pressed herself against him, reveling in the hard ridge of flesh pressing against her stomach, and his restless hands cruising down her back and over her buttocks. Yes, he did indeed know what she liked.

She felt him inching her skirt up her thighs, and delight shivered through her. When the material reached the top of her thighs, his hands still. Breaking off their kiss, he looked at her. She splayed one hand against his chest, absorbing the hard, heavy beat of his heart, the rise and fall of each ragged breath, exhilarated that she had such an effect on him. He skimmed his hands underneath her bunched-up skirt and cupped her bare bottom.

His eyes briefly slid closed. When he opened them again, the heat in his gaze nearly scorched her. "Do you have any idea how the thought of you sitting across from me, close enough to touch, wearing nothing beneath this skirt, drove me insane all evening?" He pushed her skirt higher around her waist, and his fingers played lightly over her buttocks, gently squeezing, tickling, delving, rendering her incapable of speech.

"I couldn't think of anything but you," he whispered against her lips. "Touching you. Tasting you."

He stepped forward, urging her back until her legs hit the mattress, then he pressed her gently down until she lay on the cover, her upper body supported by her elbows. He sank to his knees on the floor.

"Spread your legs for me, Jilly. Let me touch you. Taste you."

Heart pounding, she splayed her legs wider. She watched him arouse her with his fingers, caressing her with a slow, drugging, circular motion that had her undulating her hips in a silent plea for more. He kissed and nibbled and licked his way slowly up her inner thigh. The sight of his dark head nestled between her legs, his silky hair brushing over her skin, his magic touch against her sensitive, aroused flesh, all conspired to steal what remained of her control.

When he slid his hands beneath her buttocks and lifted her to his mouth, a long moan of unrestrained pleasure escaped her. She collapsed onto her back, and her eyes slid shut as she reveled in the incredible feel of his tongue and lips and fingers gliding, caressing, driving her past the edge of reason. An intense orgasm throbbed through her, wave after wave of deep release that left her breathless, limp, and utterly sated.

Matt raised his head, and stilled at the heart-stopping

sight of Jilly, flushed, mussed, skirt pushed up to her waist, thighs splayed, eyes closed, limp from pleasure. With the taste of her lingering on his tongue, he rose and quickly undressed. After rolling on a condom, he loomed over her.

"Look at me, Jilly."

She slowly opened her eyes. With their gazes locked, he entered her in one long, smooth stroke, burying himself in her silky, tight heat. He clasped her hands, entwining their fingers, then moved slowly, deliberately, withdrawing nearly all the way from her body, before gliding deep again. Her eyes darkened, then glazed with renewed passion. His mouth teased hers, licking, circling, his tongue imitating his slow strokes inside her body. He concentrated on every nuance of her body against his, her wet, velvety heat surrounding him, her heart beating against his.

He felt her tension slowly build, and he broke off their kiss, gritting his teeth to prolong their pleasure, but the battle was lost when she wrapped her legs around his hips and groaned his name. His strokes increased in pace, his hands gripped hers tighter. Burying his face against her fragrant neck, he tensed. His release shuddered through him, ripping a long, ragged groan from his chest.

A good minute passed before he found the strength to lift his head. When he did, he found himself looking down into her serious eyes. Eyes that reflected the same question that he knew shadowed his own: How were they going to ignore this when they returned to work on Tuesday?

He wanted to make a joke, lighten the mood, but he couldn't possibly. Not when he was still buried deep in her body. Not when he could feel her heartbeat pounding against his, when their fingers remained entwined, and her legs still gripped his hips.

"Wow," she finally whispered, the ghost of a smile touching her lips. "So, um, what's next on the dessert menu?"

"You can have anything you want."

Her eyes darkened. "That's the second time you've told me that."

"And you still haven't claimed your prize from our snowball fight."

"I haven't forgotten. I'm just waiting for the perfect moment."

He shifted inside her, then groaned when her inner walls squeezed him. "This feels pretty perfect to me."

"Is there a statute of limitations on claiming my prize?"

"No."

"Good. Then I'll hold off." She grinned and stretched beneath him. "Maybe wait till you trade in your Lexus for a Mercedes."

"I think you're forgetting the 'within reason' part of the deal."

"Maybe." She wriggled her hands free, then stroked her fingers down his back. "Now, about this offer that I can have anything I want next from the dessert menu—I do have a craving."

He lowered his head and ran his tongue over her plump lower lip. "If it's anything like what I'm craving, I think we're both in for a treat. Tell me what you want."

"I want you and me in the bathtub, the bubble jets massaging us with warm water, while we feed each other the offerings from that lovely dessert platter and drink that chilled champagne. Whaddaya say?"

"I say we want the same things."

11

JILLY CAME AWAKE SLOWLY. She lay on her side, the comforter pulled up to her chin. Peeking one eye open, she noted the digital numbers on the alarm clock glowing 11:43 a.m. Thanks to the heavy velvet drapes, the room remained dark, but she didn't need to see—not when she could feel so much.

Matt, lying behind her, his body touching the length of hers, his legs pressing against the back of her thighs, one strong arm wrapped around her waist, his palm cupping her breast. His deep, even breaths brushing across her nape, and his chest hair tickling her shoulders.

Her eyes drifted closed, and she remained perfectly still, drinking in the sensation of his warmth pressed against her. Images of last night danced behind her eyelids, indelible images she knew would haunt her for a very long time. Of her and Matt laughing in the jet tub, feeding each other grapes and strawberries, sipping chilled champagne, then making love while the heated water swirled around them. Then moving their indoor picnic to the bed where they indulged in the delights hidden under the silver-domed plates. She was quite certain the chef at Le Cabernet Bistro hadn't meant for his exquisitely rich chocolate mousse to be enjoyed in the ways she and Matt discovered. They'd talked and laughed and loved until they'd finally fallen asleep.

And now that Monday had arrived, their interlude was over.

This was the last time Matt would ever hold her like this. The last time she'd ever feel his skin next to hers. An aching, heavy loss filled her. Did he feel that loss, too? Her throat tightened at the prospect of pretending he meant nothing to her when she saw him at work tomorrow. Was he dreading it as well? Or would he be able to forget the intimacies that had passed between them and be "business as usual" at the office? She somehow doubted it. The way he'd looked at her, touched her, and made love to her, indicated he, too, felt some of this regret—or whatever this thing she was experiencing was called. He hadn't said so, but the emotion was there. In his eyes. In his touch. Wasn't it?

She hadn't asked. Was afraid to know. Was afraid his answer might be no, and then she'd feel like an idiot who'd let a weekend fling touch her heart instead of just her body. And if he said yes, he *did* feel the same things she did, well, that was just as frightening and unacceptable and definitely better left unsaid, for there was nowhere for such feelings to go. Nothing had changed. Once Jack Witherspoon made his decision, either Matt would be her boss, or she'd be Matt's boss. An interoffice affair under such circumstances was out of the question. Besides, their personalities just didn't mesh. Matt was definitely a take-charge guy, and she wasn't about to let any man have that power over her. What hope was there for two people equally determined to win the same prize? None. No, this was it. The end.

No sooner had the thought crossed her mind than Matt stirred behind her. His fingers kneaded her breast, hardening her nipples. She arched back, pressing more fully against him, and a purr of pleasure vibrated in her throat.

"Good morning, gorgeous," he whispered. His breath chased across her ear, shooting shivers of delight down her spine.

"Right back atcha," she murmured, reaching up and back to sift her fingers through his thick, dark hair. "Although it's almost noon." *And check-out time is one o'clock....*

Matt buried his face in her fragrant hair and ignored the mantra pumping through his brain, *this is the last time you'll touch her...the last time.* Well, he intended to make the most of it.

His hand cruised slowly down her torso, his mind visualizing the creamy skin beneath his fingers. The smattering of freckles decorating her chest. The tiny beauty mark just below her left breast. The shallow indent of her navel. He lightly bit her neck, then laved the spot with his tongue, absorbing the delicate shudder that ran through her. "Have I told you how delicious you taste?" he asked.

"Hmmmm. Not in the last several hours."

He nuzzled the skin behind her ear and breathed deep. "Or how incredible you smell? Or how soft your skin is?" His hand skimmed lower, and with a low moan, she shifted, her buttocks brushing against his erection as she spread her legs. He lightly teased her swollen, feminine folds, then slipped two fingers inside her. "How wet and tight, silky and hot are you?"

She undulated against him, and he gritted his teeth against the pleasure of her firm buttocks cradling his erection. When he slipped his fingers from her, she groaned in protest. Grabbing a condom from the stash on the nightstand, he quickly sheathed himself, then eased into her velvety heat from behind. He made leisurely love to her, savoring each slow thrust, each of her sighs, the sensation of her back pressed to his front. Her orgasm gripped him like a pulsing, velvet fist, and holding her tight against him, he buried his face against the curve of her neck and surrendered to his release. And the instant his shudders stopped, the mantra began again. *That was the last time. The last time.*

MATT STEPPED FROM THE SHOWER half an hour later and swallowed his disappointment that Jilly hadn't joined him. Feeling let down was ridiculous, especially given that she'd showered first. Their interlude was over.

Pushing aside the ache that thought brought, he quickly shaved, then packed up his toiletries, noting that Jilly's were already gone from the counter. He opened the bathroom door, and halted. Dressed in jeans, her sturdy boots, black turtleneck, her hair pulled back into its usual chignon, she looked neat, remote, sexy as hell, and he wanted nothing more than to get her undressed. Her overnight bag, laptop, and the box of flowers he'd given her all sat at her feet.

"I'm ready to leave," she said.

He swallowed to locate his voice. "Okay. I only need a few minutes—"

"I called a cab to bring me to the train station. The next train leaves in twenty minutes."

He raked his hands through his wet hair and stood there, dressed in nothing but a towel, a dozen confusing, conflicting things he wanted to say buzzing through his mind, but not knowing how to express any of them. Afraid to say anything for fear of not saying enough. Or of saying way too much.

"I'd be happy to drive you home, Jilly. In fact, I'd sort of planned, or rather hoped, to do so."

"Thank you, but I've already made my arrangements."

She didn't say *I don't need or want you making plans for*

me, but she might as well have. He suppressed the urge to yank on his hair in frustration.

"I...I think it's better this way, Matt."

His common sense knew she was right. A quick, clean goodbye here at the hotel, no messy farewells. So why did he feel so...miserable?

"It was a great weekend," she said.

"Yeah, it was."

The shadow of a smile flitted across her lips—lips whose texture and taste were permanently embedded in his brain. "So I guess I'll see you at work tomorrow."

"Tomorrow," he agreed.

She hesitated for a second, and he tensed, wondering if she was going to say something more. But what else was there to say? Nothing except—

"Goodbye, Matt."

Yeah, that's all there was left to say. And she'd said it. She reached down and picked up her things, then leaned toward him and lightly brushed her mouth across his. The scent of clean laundry wafted over him. She opened the door, and a second later she was gone, leaving him with nothing but an elusive trail of her scent, a three-day weekend filled with indelible memories, and a hollow ache around his heart.

TUESDAY MORNING, JILLY WALKED into Maxximum Advertising, her professional armor firmly welded in place. Hair pulled back into her sleekest chignon, dressed in her chocolate-brown, pinstripe, "don't mess with me" suit, her black-rimmed glasses perched on her nose, she was ready to face anything. Including Matt Davidson.

Sure, her heart was pounding, but only because she'd sprinted for the elevator. And yes, her nerves jittered, but only because she'd indulged in an extra-large coffee on the train, and all that caffeine on an empty stomach was kicking in. She just needed something to eat. Cruising by her cubicle, she plopped her briefcase on her leather chair, turned on her computer, then headed for the break room, ready to warm up the blueberry muffin she'd purchased from the corner market. Bakery bag in hand, she entered the brightly lit break room. And halted as if she'd walked into a wall.

Matt leaned against the counter, drinking from a blue, New York Mets ceramic coffee mug, perusing a folded-over page of the *Wall Street Journal*. He looked up, over the rim of his mug, and stilled. For several long seconds they stared at each other in silence. A myriad of images flashed through her mind. Matt smiling at her. Laughing with her. Kissing her. Touching her. Buried deep inside her.

Gripping her bakery bag, Jilly banished the images and forced her feet to move and her lips to curve upward, praying her smile didn't appear as tight as it felt.

"Good morning," she said, walking briskly toward the sink, slapping away the memory of how they'd awakened together yesterday morning.

"Good morning." He jerked his head toward the coffee machine. "I just put on a fresh pot."

"Great." Jilly busied herself at the sink, rinsing out her coffee cup, removing her muffin from the bag, all the while pretending she didn't notice the way his charcoal-gray suit hugged his broad shoulders and long legs. Or remember how good he looked, and felt, underneath his clothing.

"I wonder if Jack Witherspoon will contact Adam today," he said.

"I don't know. But if not today, then certainly this

week. Jack wants to launch the ad campaign as soon as possible."

From the corner of her eye, she watched him cross to the fridge. Then he walked back to her, and set the container of milk next to her cup.

"What's that for?" she asked.

"Your coffee."

Their eyes met and Jilly's insides seemed to tense and melt at the same time. Lifting her chin, she said, "You've never brought me the milk for my coffee before."

"I never knew you took milk in your coffee...before."

In the span of a heartbeat, a wealth of intimate knowledge passed between them, and she bit the insides of her cheeks in an attempt to stem the dread seeping through her. Good grief, if she couldn't even remain detached during a brief encounter in the break room, what hope did she have to survive working with him on a daily basis?

None. So it was time to buck up and get a grip. Time to forget about the intimacies they'd shared and concentrate on the fact that the object on the counter might *look* like an innocent container of milk, but it represented the personification of his take-charge personality—the trait in a man she'd spent her entire dating life avoiding.

Wiping her face clean of all expression, or at least she prayed she did, she forced her gaze to remain steady on his. "Thank you, but I'm perfectly capable of getting my own milk."

"I'm perfectly aware of that."

"I hope you plan to honor our agreement for it to be business as usual between us, Matt."

"Of course." He raised his brows. "Unless you've changed your mind?"

"No. Of course not." Really. Definitely not. "I just feel the need to remind you of our agreement."

"Because I brought you milk for your coffee?" Before she could answer, he stepped closer to her, invading her space—the space she needed to keep between them so she wouldn't reach out and touch him. She backed up, but her hips hit the counter, leaving her nowhere else to go. He halted when only a foot separated them. Leaning forward, he braced his arms on the counter, caging her in. Her heart pounded, and her brain screamed at her to move away, but her feet remained stubbornly in place. She should have been outraged at this further manifestation of his take-charge ways. And as soon as she could breath properly again, thus providing the necessary amounts of oxygen to her suddenly numb brain, she would voice her outrage. Definitely. A muscle ticked in his jaw…his clean-shaven jaw that her fingers itched to touch.

"Per our agreement, I have every intention of ignoring what happened between us as best I can," he said, in a low, tight voice, "but it's proving a bit more difficult than I'd anticipated. Unfortunately I don't operate like a light switch that can be turned off and on at will, although I dearly wish I did. As time goes on, I hope this will get easier. But in the meantime, I'd appreciate it if you'd take my word that I'm trying, and that I might mess up."

His gaze skimmed down her body before returning to hers. "Believe me, if I didn't intend to honor our agreement, you'd sure as hell know it. Because instead of giving you the damn milk, I'd kiss you. I'd tell you that I feel like hell this morning as a result of not sleeping last night because I couldn't stop thinking about you. And that I'm not looking forward to the next few days or weeks or however long it's going to take until I can be in the same room with you and not feel this...whatever the hell it is. And that instead of making small talk, I want to ask you to dinner tonight."

Jilly stood perfectly still, heart racing, all thoughts of outrage gone, mesmerized by the clear frustration simmering in his eyes. Tension and desire and heat radiated off him, and it was all she could do not to touch him. Evidently he was experiencing the same conflicted feelings and desires as she, a fact that surely should not have pleased her. But she was only human and, damn it, misery loved company.

Drawing a deep breath, she shifted sideways. His arms fell to his sides, and she quickly put some space between them. Feeling much more in control, she lifted her chin. "Yes, this is awkward, but we knew it would be. And as you said, it will hopefully get easier with each passing day. As for dinner tonight, that is impossible, not only because it would violate our agreement, but because I already have a date."

Silence swelled between them, and she had to force herself not to look away from him. *Telling him you already have a date definitely stretches the bounds of truth,* her conscience chided. She mentally duct-taped her conscience into silence. She did have a date. Sort of. So what if it was with Kate? It was hardly her fault if Matt believed she was already dating another man. In fact, if he did, that was good, right? And wasn't that the entire goal of tonight's club-hop with Kate—to find a man to date? You betcha.

A curtain seemed to drop over his expression. "Not to worry," he said, his voice devoid of emotion. "I wasn't actually going to ask you to dinner. I understand the rules." Without another word, he retrieved his coffee mug and newspaper, then left the break room. Jilly stared at the empty doorway, bit down on her bottom lip to stop its trembling, and firmly told herself that this was good.

Yeah. So then why did she feel so bad?

"HOW ABOUT THE TALL, BLOND guy standing at the end of the bar?" Kate asked over the din of pulsating music. "The one wearing the pale blue sweater?"

Jilly glanced toward the bar from the vantage point of their small corner table. She shook her head. "I prefer dark hair."

"All right. How about the guy standing next to the blond guy? He has dark hair and is definitely good-looking."

Jilly checked out the man. Yup, no doubt about it, he was dark-haired and good-looking. Strikingly so. But for all the heat he generated in her, he might as well have been a telephone pole. "Sorry. I'm not feelin' a spark."

Kate sent her an exasperated look. "Well, you might feel a spark if you'd get your butt out of that chair and go chat with someone besides me. How are we supposed to find you a man to date if the only person you'll talk to is me?"

"I like talking to you."

"Thank you. I like talking to you, too. And I bet if you gave that gorgeous man half a glance, he'd like to talk to you, also."

Jilly shrugged. "Maybe later. Right now I'd rather hear about the rest of your weekend."

"Fine. Ben and I ordered out Chinese, went over the guest list for the wedding, and enjoyed incredible sex. How about the guy in the white shirt holding the martini glass?"

Jilly flicked her gaze over him. "Hair's too long, don't like the goatee."

"He could get his hair cut and shave."

"You know what they say—never try to change a man."

Kate studied her for several long seconds, and Jilly tried her best to appear nonchalant under the scrutiny, but clearly she failed because Kate nodded.

"I understand," Kate said.

"Understand what?"

"What's the matter with all these men here. They all share the very same problem."

"Yes, they do. I'm not attracted to any of them."

"Precisely. And the reason you're not is because not one of them is Matt Davidson."

Jilly wanted to refute the statement, but it was so true, that to do so she surely risked getting sizzled by a lightning bolt. She pressed her fingers to her temples, then shook her head in frustration and defeat. "What am I going to do, Kate?"

"That depends. How strong are your feelings for him?"

"Strong. I strongly feel he's all wrong for me."

Kate looked toward the ceiling. "I meant your *feeling* feelings."

Unease trickled through Jilly's veins. "I'm...I'm not sure."

"Well, maybe *you're* not sure, but I am. Jilly, there's only one type of woman who could look at that array of beautiful men standing three deep at the bar and not see something that interested her."

Jilly shot her a look. "I'm not a lesbian."

"I know. Jilly, you're in love."

Jilly nearly spewed her margarita. "I am not."

"Of course you are. Good grief, you might as well have it tattooed on your forehead in big, neon-green letters. I suspected as much, but when you didn't even bat an eyelash at that divine, dark-haired Adonis, I knew."

"I didn't see *you* ogling the Adonis."

"Of course not. And do you know why? Because I'm *in love*." Kate leaned back and smiled triumphantly. "I rest my case."

Damn it, she needed to find herself a friend who wasn't a lawyer. Yet, the words echoed in her mind until the realization that Kate was right hit Jilly like a blow to the head. Good God, she wasn't merely attracted to Matt, she *loved* him. Loved everything about him. His smile. His laugh. His sense of humor and fun. His integrity. His work ethic. His obvious love for his family. His inability to throw a decent snowball. The way he touched her. Kissed her. Made love to her. Jilly's unease turned into full-fledged panic. A strangled sound escaped.

"What's that noise?" Kate asked.

"My emotional gears shifting without benefit of a clutch. Damn it, I can't be in love with him!"

Kate's eyes filled with sympathy. "Too late. Tell me, how did things go at work with him today?"

Jilly blew out a long breath and briefly squeezed her eyes shut. "Awful. Awkward. Even when we were nowhere near each other, I was aware of him every minute."

"And when you *were* near each other?"

"Torture. My heart beat fast, my hands turned clammy, my stomach jittered, and I wanted to remove his clothes—with my tongue."

"Oh boy. You're in love all right. Bad case."

"But I don't *want* to be in love with him. Why did I have to fall in love with *him*? He's my *co-worker* for crying out loud. And he's bossy. You know how that irritates me."

Kate hiked up her brows. "What bossy thing has he done now? Worse than arranging the facial for you?"

"Very funny. Well, he'd obviously planned to drive me home from the resort."

"Yeah, he deserves an ass-kicking, all right."

Jilly sizzled her with a scowl. "I didn't need him to drive me. I'd already called a cab."

"All right. Did he argue with you about it? Try to force you into his car?"

"Well, no."

"What else?"

The distinct feeling that she was on the losing end of this battle eased through Jilly. "He brought me the milk for my coffee in the break room this morning," she said in a small voice.

Kate laughed, then leaned forward. "Jilly, you've been so determined for so long not to allow a man to take care of you that you've become unable to distinguish 'bossy' from 'thoughtful.' So he tries to arrange things—so what? Hasn't he also deferred to your wishes?"

She reflected for several seconds, and the truth behind Kate's words dawned like the sun rising over Jilly's head. At work, Matt was definitely a take-charge guy, and it was one of the reasons he was so good at his job. She couldn't fault him for that. And away from work, while he did exhibit take-charge tendencies, they were, as Kate said, thoughtful gestures. Romantic gestures. Polite gestures. And he had on several occasions deferred to her wishes in a very gentlemanly way.

Jilly blinked. "I think maybe I was looking for and assuming he had faults that he doesn't really have."

"Of course you were."

A sensation like air streaming from an untied balloon filled Jilly. "Well, what kind of doofus does that make me?"

"You're not a doofus. You're cautious. And in this day and age, that's a good thing."

"But I still don't want to love the guy, Kate. This affair could totally screw up my career. How can I make these feelings go away?"

"It's love, Jilly, not a sinus infection."

"Hurts just as much."

"No one said love was painless. But isn't that better than feeling nothing at all?"

"I sincerely doubt it." She blew out a long breath. "Well, I guess I have three choices." Ticking them off on her fingers, she said, "One—I can continue my affair with Matt, assuming he's willing, and let the chips fall where they may."

"Pros and cons of that?"

"Pro is I'd get to be with the man I've unfortunately allowed myself to fall in love with. Con is that when the chips fall, as they inevitably will, I'll be left with a broken heart, and an impossible work situation that could derail my career."

Kate winced. "What's choice number two?"

"Stay as far away from Matt as possible and pray that my feelings will lessen over time."

"Not to discourage you, but I don't think there's enough hours in the day for all the prayers that plan would require. What's the third option?"

"Strike up a conversation with the dark-haired Adonis at the bar and hope for the best. If he can make me forget Matt for even one minute, I'm willing to give it a try." She cracked her knuckles, rolled her shoulders, then stood. "Wish me luck. I'm goin' in."

COMFORTABLY DRESSED in a beat-up Mets sweatshirt and jeans, long-neck bottle of icy beer in one hand, TV remote in the other, Matt sat in his favorite recliner and aimlessly channel surfed, trying his damnedest not to think of the one thing he couldn't erase from his mind.

He was failing completely.

He glanced at the clock: 10:00 p.m. Was she still out on her date? Probably. She was likely at some romantic restaurant right this minute, smiling at Brad the dentist. Or maybe dinner was over and they'd gone back to his place. Or her place.

His fingers tightened on the cold glass bottle, and he squeezed his eyes shut in a futile effort to banish the image of another man enjoying her company. Touching her. Kissing her. Making love to her.

Seeing her today at work had been nothing short of torture. The instant she'd appeared in the break room, he'd wanted to touch her. Throughout the remainder of the day, it had required an incredible amount of effort to get any work done. Yet even when he'd managed to do so, part of him had always been on "Jilly alert."

He heaved a long sigh and shook his head at his own folly. Clearly he harbored deep-seated, masochistic tendencies to allow himself to get involved with another coworker. How many freakin' times did he need to make *that* mistake?

His even bigger mistake had been his gross miscalculation in his ability to forget Jilly. Had he actually believed he could share a weekend of sexual fun and games with her, then simply place the entire affair into a neat little file labeled "over and done with"? Good God, he needed to have his head examined. Oh, he'd known some awkwardness would enter into the mix, but he'd figured they'd both just move on.

Problem was, he had absolutely no desire to move on. And he definitely didn't want her to move on. No, he sure as hell hadn't counted on feeling like this. So...dismembered. Like someone had ripped out his heart, and grabbed his soul while they were at it, then dumped them both in the East River. He thunked his head back against the soft leather headrest. What the hell was wrong with him?

I'll tell you what's wrong, his inner voice said, coughing to life, *although why you can't figure it out yourself is beyond me. Jeez, for a smart guy, you've dropped the ball this time. You're in love, you jerk.*

Matt's eyes popped open and he sat up as if a giant spring were attached to his ass. In love? No, surely he couldn't be *that* masochistically insane.

But the words *you're in love* reverberated through his brain like a death march, and as much as he wanted to refute them, he couldn't. He'd made the same damn mistake all over again—falling in love with a woman he worked with—a situation that had disaster written all over it. If he'd thought indulging in a brief affair with Jilly was unwise, falling in love with her took home the Olympic gold for stupidity.

He dropped the remote and dragged his hand down his face, trying to stave off the panic nipping at him. *Maybe this isn't love,* his brain stated hopefully. *Maybe it's just a case of severe lust gone crazy.*

But as much as that would offer a great relief, his heart instantly rejected the suggestion. This wasn't just lust. He knew what mere physical attraction felt like, and what he felt for Jilly went *waaaaay* beyond a mere wanting to get her naked—although he couldn't deny that he wanted that too.

No, there was no doubt he loved her, damn it. He'd

loved Tricia, yet what he'd felt for her paled to beige in comparison to the feelings and emotions Jilly inspired. He cared for her, wanted her—both in and out of bed— with an intensity that stunned him. Jilly was simply more important than anything else.

Looking back, he realized that he'd harbored a latent attraction to her for a long time. Over the past year, he'd enjoyed their verbal sparring matches at the office, and matching wits with her over ad campaigns. Liked that the challenge of competing with her brought out the best in his work. Admired her professionalism, even though he hadn't entirely trusted her, thanks to his experience with Tricia.

But Jilly had proven her integrity and had won not only his trust and admiration, but his heart—and he had so *not* been looking to give that away. Especially to some-one with whom he shared the predicament that one of them was going to be the other's boss.

Well, he might not have been planning to fall in love, but fall in love he had. Now he just had to decide what the hell he was going to do about it. And while he had no clue, he did know one thing—sitting in his apartment while she was on a date with some other guy was simply not going to work. It was time to make some plans.

12

JILLY SPENT THE REMAINDER of the week doing everything in her power to stop thinking about Matt. She devoted her hours at the office to working on current projects with single-minded determination. She stayed in her cubicle, studiously avoiding the break room. On Wednesday morning, she caught several glimpses of Matt—and each time her heart performed a somersault—but then was granted a reprieve as he spent most of Wednesday and all of Thursday out of the office with clients. Unfortunately "out of sight" did not translate into "out of mind."

Instead of returning to her quiet home after work on Wednesday and Thursday, she'd dragged Kate to several more clubs. With the same determination that guided her days, she danced with bankers and stockbrokers, chatted with accountants and salesmen, laughed with lawyers and techies. And hated every single minute of it.

Plus, she tortured herself wondering what Matt was doing while she hit the clubs. Was he doing the same? Was he dancing with someone else? Touching someone else? Making love to someone else?

By the time Friday rolled around, she was ready to admit defeat. She and Kate, accompanied by Ben, were supposed to make the club rounds again after work, but after three days of that, Jilly knew she couldn't stomach another such outing. She'd tried to forget Matt by meeting someone else, but there simply wasn't anyone else she wanted to meet. Her plan to banish him from her mind and push her feelings for him aside was a spectacular failure. Damn it, the man she wanted—the *only* man she wanted—was Matt. And it was time she did something about it.

But what? The thought of admitting her feelings gave her the willies. Yet the thought of remaining apart from him gave her even worse willies. Surely he'd turn green and head for the hills if she blurted out, "I've fallen in love with you." Of course, there wasn't any law that said she had to admit *all* of her feelings. She could just admit, "I find you devastatingly attractive and want to resume our affair." Her body and hormones were certainly all for that solution. *Oh, sure, you guys are all for it,* her heart balked, *but I'm the one who risks being flattened like a bug.*

Good grief, it was true. Indulging in an affair when one party—and *only* one party—was in love did not bode well for the party in love. And that was her.

Before she could give the matter further thought, her phone rang with the buzz that indicated an interoffice call. She lifted the receiver, and her boss's deep voice greeted her, requesting she come to his office.

"It's regarding Jack Witherspoon and the ARC account," Adam said.

With butterflies flapping in her stomach, Jilly replaced the phone on its cradle, then hurried down the hall toward Adam's office. Adam's bland tone hadn't provided any clues as to whether he was about to impart good news or bad news. But either way, her career and life were about to change. She would either walk out of Adam's office as Matt's boss—or Matt's underling.

As she approached Adam's secretary's desk, Debra smiled. "Go right on in, Jilly. He's expecting you."

Forgoing the urge to press her hands to her jittery mid-section, she knocked once, then entered. Her knees trembled a bit as she crossed the expanse of pale blue carpet, and she gratefully sank into the leather chair across from Adam.

He steepled his hands and regarded her with a grave expression that engulfed Jilly with a huge wave of foreboding.

"Well, Jilly, there's no easy way to say this, so I'm just going to say it. I'm afraid you didn't get the ARC account."

Adam's words buzzed through her brain like a swarm of angry hornets. Disappointment lodged a golf-ball size lump in her throat. Damn. She'd wanted that account so much. Had worked hard for it, and had coveted the next step in her career that winning the account would have provided—not to mention the financial security the bonus would have brought her. Yet, mixed in with her disappointment was an unmistakable surge of happiness for Matt. His campaign and ideas for ARC were excellent, and if she couldn't have the account, she was glad he'd have it.

Clearing her throat to dislodge the lump, she said, "Naturally I'm disappointed, but Matt's ideas for ARC were innovative and cutting edge. I know he'll do a great job for ARC."

Adam nodded. "Yes, I'm sure he would have—as I'm sure you would have—had Jack Witherspoon chosen either of you, which unfortunately he did not."

Jilly stared. "I beg your pardon?"

Adam spread his hands in a "what can I say?" gesture. "In spite of the weekend at the winery, and putting my two best people after him—"

"You mean *pitting* your two best people after him," Jilly observed archly.

Adam shot her an unrepentant grin. "I did what I thought was best to increase Maxximum's odds of winning the account. Unfortunately we didn't win."

"Have you told Matt yet?"

"No. Ladies first."

"Who did Jack decide to go with?"

"A new exec with our chief competitor, the Enterprise Agency," Adam reported, "who recently joined Enterprise from the Opus Agency in L.A. A woman named Carol Webber."

Jilly froze at the familiar name. "Carol Webber? Have you met her?"

"Yes. Just this morning. Jack introduced us."

"Is she a tall, slim, attractive blonde with a small beauty mark above her lip?"

Adam nodded. "That's her." He shot her a curious look. "You know her?"

"Unfortunately, yes." Jilly quickly filled Adam in on Carol Webber, the "nurse" who'd charmed Jack at the winery. "Obviously she found out Jack was going to be there, and she showed up with the intention of luring him away from Maxximum," Jilly fumed.

"And she succeeded."

"I wonder what Jack's reaction was when she told him she wasn't really a nurse?"

"Clearly he wasn't all that devastated," Adam said dryly. He shrugged. "It's unfortunate, but we've both been in this business long enough to know that playing dirty often reaps results. And while I'm not happy about losing out on ARC's account, it's over and done with, and there are other potential clients to consider—which is the next thing I want to discuss with you. Millenium Airways has just signed on with us, and I'm looking for someone to head up their campaign. There's a sizable bonus involved, not to mention some free flights on the airline. There'd also be a lot of traveling involved with the account. You interested?"

Interested? In heading up a prestigious account like Millenium Airways? A bonus? Free flights? Travel? She'd be crazy *not* to be interested. It sounded incredible. So why was she hesitating? Yet even as she asked herself the question, she knew the answer.

"Listen, Adam, as much as I appreciate the opportunity, I think you should give the Millenium account to Matt."

Adam shot her a hawklike look. "Why is that?"

"Because he'd do a great job. I recall him once mentioning that he worked on Global Airways' last campaign at his previous firm, so he has experience with the airline industry. And even though Jack Witherspoon didn't choose Maxximum, Matt's ideas for ARC were brilliant. Personally, I think Jack made a huge mistake."

"Are you telling me that you think Jack should have chosen Matt's ideas over yours?" There was no mistaking the surprise in Adam's tone.

"I think we both came up with excellent ideas, but there was a simplicity to Matt's that really appealed to me. He's very talented." She smiled. "I am, too. But I think Matt is a better choice for Millenium Airways, therefore, I respectfully decline."

Adam's narrowed gaze seemed to cut right through her, and Jilly experienced the uncomfortable sensation that he could divine her thoughts. "Something happen last weekend I should know about, Jilly?"

"No. I just believe in assigning the best person to the job for the good of the company. Ninety-nine percent of the time, I think I'm the right person. In this particular case, however, I think Matt is."

"Well, I'll certainly take that under advisement." Adam stood, indicating their meeting was over. Jilly rose, shook his hand, then exited the office. She walked quickly to her cubicle where she gathered her overcoat, laptop and briefcase, then headed toward the bank of elevators. She had a meeting with a client in thirty minutes, but her thoughts were far away from the new ad campaign she was about to present. No, all she could think about was Matt, and what a great job he would do for Millenium Airways.

By the time Jilly left her client, it was nearly six o'clock. Since she was only three blocks from Penn station, she decided not to return to Maxximum's offices, but go directly home. She'd already called Kate and canceled their club hop. She was tired and her feet hurt. All she wanted to do was strip off her suit, throw on her rattiest sweats, and dig into the double chocolate brownie fudge ice cream beckoning her.

During both the short walk to Penn, then her thirty-minute Long Island Railroad train ride, she thought about Matt. Good grief, there could be no doubt that she loved the guy. If she didn't, she never would have done such an unprecedented thing as decline Adam's offer to head up the Millenium Airways account and suggest Matt for the position. But Matt deserved it. And he really was the best man for the job.

He's also the best man for you, her inner voice stated emphatically during the short drive home from the train station to her modest, Cape Cod house. Jilly heaved out a long sigh. Yes, he was. And over the course of this weekend, she planned to apply herself to formulating a plan of action for convincing Matt to resume their affair. Surely it shouldn't prove *too* difficult. He'd seemed open to the idea at the beginning of the week. Yes, being with him, and having to endure the eventual end of their affair would be painful, but, damn it, not being with him was already painful—so why not suffer *with* him instead of alone? One thing was for sure—it was time to cash in her chips and claim her prize. And as ill-advised as it might be, she wanted Matt for her prize.

She turned onto her quiet, tree-lined street. Holiday lights twinkled in windows, forcibly reminding her that tomorrow was Christmas Eve. The remnants of last weekend's snowfall coated the lawns with a blanket of white, bringing to mind a vivid, aching image of her snowball fight with Matt.

She slowed as she drew closer to her house, peering through the darkness at the black car—a very familiar black car—parked in her driveway. Her heart skipped a beat, then thumped hard.

With her insides quivering, she pulled in behind the Lexus. Almost immediately, the driver's door opened, and Matt climbed out. Her headlights played over him, dressed in a dark wool overcoat, a Burberry plaid scarf tucked around his neck, one hand jammed into his coat pocket while the other clutched a plain, brown shopping bag. He looked tall and beautiful and serious and good enough to eat. And *here.*

But *why* was he here? Well, she certainly wouldn't find out sitting in the car, and she definitely wanted to know. Drawing a bracing breath meant to calm her jangling nerves—and which utterly failed—she turned off her ignition. *Be calm, be cool.* Great advice. Only problem was she felt extremely *un*calm and *un*cool.

Grabbing her purse and other belongings, she slid

from the car, then bumped the door closed with her hip. Forcing a display of nonchalance that deserved not only an Oscar but an Emmy and a Golden Globe as well, she said, "Well, this is a surprise."

"Not an unpleasant one, I hope."

Jilly cocked a brow. "Depends on why you're here."

"I'd be happy to tell you—" his gaze drifted toward the house "—if you'd like to invite me in." When she hesitated he added, "It's kinda cold out here, and I forgot my gloves."

Another image of their snowball fight flashed through her mind. He'd forgotten his gloves then, too. The image was followed immediately by a mental picture of them kissing in the snow.

"How did you know where I live?"

"Well, I'd love to dazzle you with my brilliance and say it was very complicated and required a great deal of detective work, but actually I just looked you up in the Nassau county phone book."

"Ah. Mystery solved. How long have you been waiting?"

"About an hour."

"And how did you know I'd even come home tonight?"

Something flashed in his eyes. "I didn't," he said softly. "But I hoped you would."

Surely he had to hear her heart beating. She could hear the *thump, thump, thump* in her own ears. And the rapid puffs of cold vapor emanating from between her lips were surefire giveaways of her uncalm, uncool state.

Commanding her legs to move and her eyeballs to quit gawking at him, she nodded toward the cement path leading to her front door. "Well, I don't want to be responsible for you freezing to death out here, so c'mon in."

A quick grin flashed across his handsome features and he fell into step beside her. "Thanks."

Half a minute later, they stepped into the small, ceramic-tiled foyer. Jilly flicked on a pair of switches that illuminated the front picture window with tiny, blinking holiday lights, and lit up the small Christmas tree set in the corner.

Matt yanked his gaze away from Jilly before he gave into the overwhelming urge to mess up her perfect chignon, and instead focused his attention on the simple, yet tasteful den furnishings. Pale walls, cushy sectional sofa, glass-topped coffee table adorned with a pile of magazines, television and stereo set into an attractive oak entertainment center. Framed photos were scattered on end tables, and several 8x10s hung on the wall, all depicting Jilly with an attractive woman who was clearly her mother, and a smiling man—based on the resemblance, obviously her father.

The room reflected so many of the things he loved about her—it was neat, comfortable, warm and inviting. Beyond the den he saw the unlit eat-in kitchen.

"Nice place," he said with a smile that he hoped didn't announce his nervousness.

"Thank you. It's a great neighborhood, and I was lucky enough to buy the house just before the Long Island housing prices increased from 'insane' to 'completely insane.'" She accepted his coat and hung it in a small closet near the door. "I rent out the upstairs, which helps considerably with the mortgage. My tenant, Mrs. Peterson, is a gem. She's a widow, and I inherited her when I bought the house."

"Did I take her parking spot?"

"No. She's in Florida for the holidays, visiting her son. I really miss her. Having her here makes living alone not so...alone."

"Yeah," he said softly, his gaze roaming over her face, then resting on her beautiful lips. "Alone stinks."

He heard her swallow. Then she closed the closet and nodded at the shopping bag he still gripped. "What's in there?"

"I'll show you in a minute."

"Okay." Her hand swept toward the sofa. "Make yourself at home. Can I get you something?"

His gaze flitted over her no-nonsense black suit, and a dozen things she could get him instantly streaked through his mind. He forced himself to shake his head. "No, thanks."

She moved to the sofa and sat, then indicated he should do the same. He settled himself, leaving several feet between them on the overstuffed cushion, and placed his shopping bag near his feet. Her gaze darted to her watch, and his stomach clenched. "Am I keeping you from something?" he asked. *Or someone?*

"No. I was just wondering why you were here—and how you managed to arrive before me, especially driving from Manhattan with the crazy Friday-night traffic and all the Christmas shoppers on top of that."

"I left the office early. In fact, I left the office right after I spoke to Adam."

She blew out a long breath. "Pretty unbelievable about 'nurse' Carol Webber pulling in ARC's account, huh?"

"Actually, having been the victim of such under-handed tactics before, I unfortunately find it quite believable. Sickeningly so." Reaching out, he clasped her hand, cradling it between his palms. Her eyes widened slightly at the gesture, but she didn't pull away. Warmth raced up his arm at the feel of her soft skin, and he squelched the urge simply to yank her into his arms and kiss her until neither one of them could think straight. He hoped that would happen. But there were things that needed to be said first.

"I have a confession to make, Jilly. There were times, before our weekend at the winery, when I suspected *you* might use such underhanded tactics, and I want you to know I'm sorry for that."

She raised a brow. "Actually, Matt, I think there were times *at* the winery when you thought I might use more than my creativity to land a client."

"You're right. But I learned very quickly that I was dead wrong. In fact, I learned a great deal last weekend. Would you like to know what?" Her pulse jumped beneath his fingers, giving him hope that she was not as calm as she appeared.

"If you'd like to tell me."

"Oh, I would. When I started at Maxximum, I immediately pegged you as the person to beat. You were talented and beautiful, and I buried my instant attraction— an attraction I refused to admit even to myself—by thinking of you as an Ice Princess. And my rival. I realize now that I was subconsciously trying to win back what was stolen from me at my previous job."

He shook his head at his own foolishness. "But I learned during our weekend away that I couldn't have been more wrong. In an industry filled with vipers and sharks, you restored my faith that there are still people who possess integrity and a sense of fair play." He brushed his thumbs over the back of her hand. "I also learned that you have the most beautiful smile I've ever seen. I learned that I could laugh again and trust again. I learned that it's somehow possible for a woman to not only possess beauty and brains, but a wicked sense of humor, the softest skin I've ever imagined, a killer throwing arm, and for her to smell better than anyone on the planet."

A shaky smile pulled up one corner of her mouth. "How can you say that—have you *met* everyone on the planet?"

"I don't need to. I just know. In here." He laid one hand over his rapidly beating heart. "I learned that the last week without you was torture, and that the thought of facing another day, let alone another week, like this past one is just impossible."

Jilly's breath caught at his softly spoken words. Clearly Matt wanted to pick up their affair where they'd left off. This was exactly what she wanted—right? Yeah. She should be turning cartwheels. Except for that huge brick wall looming on the horizon labeled *The End of the Affair* into which she would eventually crash. Still, he'd been honest about his misconceptions about her, and she owed him nothing less than the same.

Drawing a bracing breath, she said, "I also have a confession to make. While I'd admired your talent from day one, I'd labeled you the sort of bossy, take-charge kind of guy who raised my hackles and whom I've always avoided like a case of the hives. But I learned that there's a difference between taking charge and being thoughtful—that just because you wanted to do something for me didn't mean you were trying to take over."

"Seems like even though we knew each other for a year, we didn't find out the important stuff until last weekend." He brushed his fingertips over her cheek, and she had to grit her teeth to keep from purring like a kitten at his touch. "Jilly, Adam told me what you did—turning

down the Millenium Airways account, telling him to offer it to me instead."

She cleared her throat. "I thought Adam would keep
that information to himself."

"That was probably his intention. He didn't tell me until after he'd offered me the account and I turned it down
and deferred it to you."

Good thing her jaw was permanently attached to her
face or it would have plunked right onto the floor. "You
turned down the chance to head up the new Millenium
Airways campaign? Are you nuts?"

"That's an odd question from someone who did the exact same thing."

His dark blue gaze searched hers with such intensity,
she had to press her thighs together to keep from squirm-
ing. "Well, I had my reasons," she said.

"I'd love to know what they were."

Because I love you and I wanted you to have the account.
"Because I honestly believe, with your previous airline
campaign experience, you're better qualified to handle
the account." Yeah, that, too.

He shook his head, clearly bemused. "Your generosity
amazes and humbles me." Again his gaze probed hers.
"Is that the only reason, Jilly?"

"Yup." At least it was the only one she was willing to
share at the moment. Something that looked like disappointment flashed in his eyes. His thumb brushed over
the back of her hand, and she battled to ignore the tingles
dancing up her arm. "Me declining in your favor makes
sense due to your prior experience," she said, "but what
possible reason could *you* have for bowing out and recommending me instead?"

"Because I think you're brilliant. Creative. The epitome of professionalism. Because I respect and admire

you. You've been at Maxximum longer than me, and I think you deserve it more than I do. And I wanted you to have the opportunity you deserve."

Warmth spread through her at his praise. "You're going to make me blush." No sooner had the words passed her lips than she felt heat suffusing her cheeks.

He reached out and touched his fingertips to her flaming skin, chuckling softly. "That's amazing. You say you're going to blush, and it happens as if on cue. Like the Disney animators were standing by, paintbrushes in hand."

His words only served to heat her face further. "Sorry. I can't help it."

"Don't apologize. It's lovely. Refreshing. And incredibly sexy."

Jilly's heart tripped over itself—at his words, and at the unmistakable desire simmering in his eyes. Flustered, she asked, "With each of us recommending the other, I wonder what Adam plans to do?"

His brows raised. "You don't know?"

"No...but it sounds like you do."

"'Fraid so. He gave the Millenium account to David Garrett."

Jilly stared. "David Garrett? The new hire?"

"That's the one. Adam thought it would be good experience for him and, unlike us, David jumped at the chance."

After taking several seconds to digest the information, Jilly shook her head. "Well, ain't that a kick in the ass."

He laughed. "It certainly is." His expression sobered. "Jilly, there's something else I want to discuss with you. The reason I came here tonight was to let you know that I want to—"

The shrill ring of the telephone cut off Matt's words,

and Jilly bit back the frustrated *aaargh!* that rose to her lips. Damn, it was supposed to be "saved by the bell," not "cursed by the bell." She debated just letting the answering machine pick up, but on the off chance that it might be a message she wouldn't want Matt to overhear—like Kate calling from a club to tell her that she was missing out on a slew of eligible hunks—she decided she'd better pick up.

"Excuse me for just a moment," she murmured, rising to pick up the receiver in the kitchen.

Matt watched her leave the room, then raked his hands through his hair and sizzled a death stare toward the unseen phone. Talk about crappy timing. Jeez. Nothing worse or more painful than a case of *propositionus interruptus.*

While she was gone, he nervously leafed through an entertainment magazine from her coffee table collection, trying not to strain to make out the low murmur of her words drifting from the kitchen. When she returned five minutes later, he abandoned the magazine. She plopped down on the cushion next to him, a bemused expression on her face.

"Have you ever noticed," she said, "that whenever something bad happens, the universe somehow manages to right itself by making something good happen?"

Thinking about how Tricia had been a bad thing for him, and Jilly was such a good thing, he answered, "As a matter of fact I have noticed that."

"Well, it's been proven true once again. You'll never believe who that was on the phone."

"Based on your expression, I'm guessing it was the folks at Publishers Clearing House and you're their newest millionaire?"

"No." She flashed a grin. "Although that would be

great. It was Joe, that nice man we met at Galini Vineyards."

Matt's brows shot up. "What did he want? Did you win a free bottle of wine in his monthly drawing?"

"No, and all I can say is it's a good thing you're sitting down. Turns out Joe's last name is none other than Galini. He doesn't just work the winery—he *owns* the place." Excitement all but glowed from her. "But the incredible part is that he also owns Tribiletto Vineyards in Italy."

Matt simply stared. "Tribiletto, as in *the* Tribiletto Vineyards—one of the foremost wineries in the world?"

"The very same. He left the day-to-day operations of Tribiletto to his sons, and started Galini Vineyards as his pet project, hoping to get a foothold in the United States. He called to say that he was very impressed with us—he liked our 'sense of fun and sincerity.' He's looking to go national with the local Galini label, and wants to tie it in with the Tribiletto label. What he needs is a good ad campaign, and he asked if we would be interested in meeting him for lunch next Wednesday at the Trigali Grill on Fifth Avenue—his company owns the restaurant, by the way, and he said it could also use some updating in its advertising." She was practically bouncing in her seat. "Think of the business this will bring to Maxximum! How's *that* for a rebound from David Garrett getting the Millenium account?"

"I'd say the universe has definitely been realigned. Well, except for one thing."

"Oh? What's that?"

"You and me."

She went perfectly still. "You and me?"

"Yeah. I'm afraid we're still off-kilter. But as I was about to tell you before the phone rang, I want to fix that."

"What did you have in mind?"

He entwined their fingers and gave her hand a light squeeze, encouraged when she squeezed him back. "About our affair...how would you feel about continuing it?"

An expression that morphed from relief to unease flickered across her face. "I don't think we can deny that doing so would make working together...difficult—"

"Exactly," he broke in, unable to hide his relief. "Which is why I don't think we should continue our affair."

Jilly felt as if she'd been stabbed through the heart. His words echoed through her mind, filling her with a hurt unlike anything she'd ever before experienced. And he looked...*happy?* Forcing a breath into lungs that felt as if they'd been steamrolled, she murmured, "I...see." A total lie, because she didn't see at all. "Then why are you here?"

"To give you this." He reached into his shopping bag and pulled out a wrapped box the size of a paperback book, only deeper. Handing her the package, he said, "Open it."

Hoping he wouldn't notice her shaking fingers, she untied the bow. He didn't want to continue their affair, but he'd driven all the way to her house and brought her a present? Good grief, and they said *women* were hard to figure out?

Setting the ripped wrapping paper on the coffee table, she opened the gift box, then pushed aside several layers of gold tissue paper to reveal a hand-size ceramic statue of a snowman. A snowman holding an arc of mini snowballs. Jilly's eyes goggled as she read the message spelled out on those little white balls: I Love You.

Certain she'd developed a freakishly sudden need for

reading glasses, she carefully lifted the statue from its nest of tissue, then turned it toward the light. She sucked in a sharp breath. Holy smokes, it really *did* read I Love You.

Her gaze swiveled to his. "I don't understand."

He raked his hands through his hair. "Damn. Not the three words I was hoping for." He studied her face, and clearly she looked as stunned as she felt because he said, "I've surprised you."

"*Surprised* doesn't even begin to describe what I'm feeling." Hope raced through her, barreling over her confusion. "I mean I don't understand how one minute you can say you don't want to continue our affair, yet in the next give me this. What do you mean?"

He shifted closer to her, then cupped her face between his hands. "I mean I love you. With all my heart." He leaned forward and kissed her so softly, so tenderly, with such restrained passion that Jilly's insides turned to syrup. When he pulled back, she had to struggle to catch her breath. Who the heck had stolen all the oxygen from the room?

His serious gaze searched hers. "You said that surprised doesn't begin to describe what you're feeling. Any chance you'd like to deal me in on what you *are* feeling?"

Jilly looked at him, so earnest and handsome, his heart in his eyes. And the floodgates of her own heart simply opened. He'd laid his cards on the table, and it was time for her to do the same. "I feel that I haven't been able to stop thinking about you for so much as a minute. I feel that you're all the things I've ever wanted in a man, all tied up in an incredible package. And I feel like the luckiest woman on the planet because I just found out that the man I love loves me back."

He briefly squeezed his eyes shut and murmured

something that sounded like *thank you, God.* When he opened his eyes, he smiled. "And just how do you know that you're the luckiest woman on the planet? Have you *met* every woman on the planet?"

"I don't need to. I just know." Pressing her hand over the spot where her heart slapped frantically against her ribs, she perfectly mimicked his earlier response. "In here."

"You love me."

She turned her face and pressed a kiss against his palm, which still rested against her cheek. "Very much."

"You have no idea how glad I am to hear that." He nodded toward the snowman's box. "There's something else in there."

"More presents?"

"'Tis the season, you know."

As if in a daze, Jilly set her snowman on the table, then fingered through the tissue paper until she found a small silver key. Holding it aloft, she asked, "What is this—the key to your heart?"

"Something like that." Again Matt reached into his shopping bag then gently placed the item he withdrew onto her lap.

She stared at the shoebox-size metal strongbox, completely mystified. "What's this?"

"It's the best strongbox on the market, completely fireproof, and virtually indestructible. A must-have for hiding all those valuables you don't want to risk falling into the wrong hands."

Okay, so it wasn't the most romantic of Christmas gifts, and clearly he was the sort of guy who preferred to buy his holiday presents at the hardware store rather than Victoria's Secret, but she could live with that. Practicality was good. She smiled. "Thank you."

"You're welcome. But don't thank me until you open it."

Jilly's heart tripped over itself. Clasping the key, she inserted it into the silver lock. Then drawing a deep breath, she lifted the lid.

Everything in her stilled as she stared at the contents. The entire bottom of the strongbox was covered with a layer of chocolate-covered marshmallows. White chocolate letters, scrawled across the top of each marshmallow, spelled out the question, *Will You Marry Me?*

Jilly squeezed her eyes shut. Good grief, she really *did* need those reading glasses. But when she reopened her eyes, the message, incredibly, remained. Tears misted her eyes, and her bottom lip trembled. This man...this wonderful, generous, sweet, kind, romantic, beautiful man was going to be the death of her. But, wow, what a way to go.

She raised her gaze to his, noting how completely frazzled and anxious he looked. Clearing her throat, she said in a conspiratorial whisper, "It would appear that the guy at the candy store really, *really* likes me."

His eyes widened with an expression bordering on panic. "The guy in the candy store didn't write that message—*I* did!"

Guilt slapped her for teasing him. The poor guy really looked worried. "I know, Matt. I was only kidding."

"I'll have you know that I made those chocolate marshmallows all by myself. Melted the chocolate and everything. And let me tell you, I am to cooking what Julia Child is to Sumo wrestling. I set off the damn smoke alarm—twice—and that chocolate gets *hot*." He held up his index finger. "Look. I got a blister."

Deeply touched and more than a little amused, she

grasped his hand and brought it her mouth, bestowing a gentle kiss on his injured fingertip. "Better?"

His expression relaxed, but he was clearly not ready for her to abandon her ministrations, because he shook his head. "I think I need some more TLC. *Lots* of TLC. Proposing is very exhausting, traumatic, and harrowing work. Especially the part when you're, ahem, waiting for an answer."

Dear God, he really did look worried. "So this is what you meant when you said we shouldn't continue our affair?"

He lightly grasped her shoulders, then leaned forward until their foreheads touched. "I don't just want to have an affair with you, Jilly. I love you and want to share my life with you. Not for just a few weeks or months, but forever. As husband and wife." He leaned back and Jilly looked into his eyes, which were so serious and intense and filled with love. For her. "Will you marry me?"

A sense of completeness, of happiness, unlike anything she'd ever known, suffused her. Matt didn't want to control her life—he wanted to share it. "I want all those same things, Matt," she whispered. "Yes. I'll marry you."

Anything else she might have thought to say was lost as his lips covered hers in a kiss filled with love and passion and promise for the future. By the time he lifted his head, she was breathing hard, and thankful she was sitting down because she'd lost all sensation in her knees.

"There's one more thing in my shopping bag," Matt said, a hint of deviltry gleaming in his eyes. He reached in, then handed her a sprig of fresh mistletoe.

Jilly laughed and twirled the sprig between her fingers. "Hmmm. I think I'm finally ready to claim my prize."

"Oh? What do you want?"

"I want the three of us—you, me, and Mr. Mistletoe—
to retire to my bedroom and see what sort of Christmas
mischief we can get into."

He pretended to ponder her proposal. "Can we bring
your chocolate-covered marshmallows?"

"Absolutely. Whaddaya say, handsome?"

"I say Merry Christmas and bring on the mischief,
sweetheart."

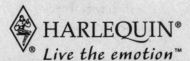

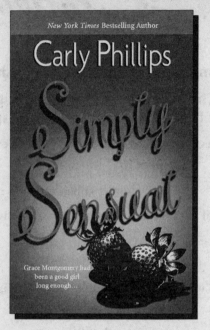
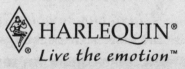

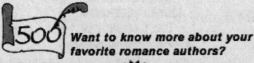

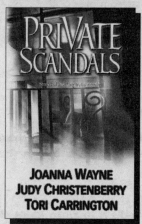
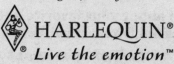

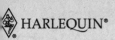

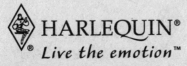

HARLEQUIN®
INTRIGUE®

Our unique brand of high-caliber romantic suspense just cannot be contained. And to meet our readers' demands, Harlequin Intrigue is expanding its publishing lineup to include **SIX** breathtaking titles every month!

___

Here's what we have in store for you:

___

❑ A trilogy of **Heartskeep** stories by Dani Sinclair

❑ More great **Bachelors at Large** books featuring sexy, single cops

❑ Plus outstanding contributions from your favorite Harlequin Intrigue authors, such as Amanda Stevens, B.J. Daniels and Gayle Wilson

MORE variety.
MORE pulse-pounding excitement.
MORE of your favorite authors and series.
Every month.

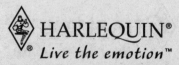

HARLEQUIN®
Live the emotion™

Visit us at www.tryIntrigue.com

HI4TO6B

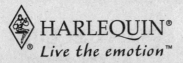